CHRISTMAS WITH HER MILLIONAIRE BOSS

BY

BARBARA WALLACE

MILLS & BOON

First published in Great Britain 2017
by Mills & Boon, an imprint of HarperCollins*Publishers*
1 London Bridge Street, London, SE1 9GF

Large Print edition 2018

© 2017 Barbara Wallace

ISBN: 978-0-263-07349-2

MIX
Paper from
responsible sources
FSC C007454

This book is produced from independently certified
FSC™ paper to ensure responsible forest management.
For more information visit www.harpercollins.co.uk/green.

Printed and bound in Great Britain
by CPI Group (UK) Ltd, Croydon, CR0 4YY

For Peter and Andrew,
who put up with a stressed-out writer
trying to juggle too many balls at one time.
You two are awesome, and I couldn't ask
for a better husband and son.

CHAPTER ONE

OH, WHAT FRESH hell was this?

A pair of ten-foot nutcrackers smiled down at him with giant white grins that looked capable of snapping an entire chestnut tree in half—let alone a single nut. Welcome to Fryberg's Trains and Toys read the red-and-gold banner clutched in their wooden hands. Where It's Christmas All Year Round.

James Hammond shuddered at the thought.

He was the only one though, as scores of children dragged their parents by the hand past the nutcracker guards and toward the Bavarian castle ahead, their shouts of delight echoing in the crisp Michigan air. One little girl, winter coat flapping in the wind, narrowly missed running into him, so distracted was she by the sight ahead of her.

"I see Santa's Castle," he heard her squeal.

Only if Santa lived in northern Germany and

liked bratwurst. The towering stucco building, with its holly-draped ramparts and snow-covered turrets looked like something out of a Grimm's fairy tale. No one would ever accuse Ned Fryberg of pedaling a false reality, that's for sure. It was obvious that his fantasy was completely unattainable in real life. Unlike the nostalgic, homespun malarkey Hammond's Toys sold to the public.

The popularity of both went to show that people loved their Christmas fantasies, and they were willing to shovel boatloads of money in order to keep them alive.

James didn't understand it, but he was more than glad to help them part with their cash. He was good at it too. Some men gardened and grew vegetables. James grew his family's net worth. And Fryberg's Toys, and its awful Christmas village—a town so named for the Fryberg family—was going to help him grow it even larger.

"Excuse me, sir, but the line for Santa's trolley starts back there." A man wearing a red toy soldier's jacket and black busby pointed behind James's shoulder. In an attempt to control traffic flow, the store provided transportation around the grounds via a garishly colored "toy" train. "Trains leave every five minutes. You won't have too long a wait.

"Or y-you could w-w-walk," he added.

People always tended to stammer whenever James looked them in the eye. Didn't matter if he was trying to be intimidating or not. They simply did. Maybe because, as his mother once told him, he had the same cold, dead eyes as his father. He'd spent much of his youth vainly trying to erase the similarity. Now that he was an adult, he'd grown not to accept his intimidating glower, but embrace it. Same way he embraced all his other unapproachable qualities.

"That depends," he replied. "Which mode is more efficient?"

"Th-that would depend upon on how fast a walker you are. The car makes a couple of stops beforehand, so someone with…with long legs…" The soldier, or whatever he was supposed to be, let the sentence trail off.

"Then walking it is. Thank you."

Adjusting his charcoal-gray scarf tighter around his neck, James turned and continued on his way, along the path to Fryberg's Christmas Castle. The faster he got to his meeting with Belinda Fryberg, the sooner he could lock in his sale and fly back to Boston. At least there, he only had to deal with Christmas one day of the year.

"What did you say?"

"I said, your Christmas Castle has a few years of viability in it, at best."

Noelle hated the new boss.

She'd decided he rubbed her the wrong way when he glided into Belinda's office like a cashmere-wearing shark. She disliked him when he started picking apart their operations. And she loathed him now that he'd insulted the Christmas Castle.

"We all know the future of retail is online," he continued. He uncrossed his long legs and shifted his weight. Uncharitable a thought as it might be, Noelle was glad he'd been forced to squeeze his long, lanky frame into Belinda's office furniture. "The only reason your brick-and-mortar store has survived is because it's basically a tourist attraction."

"What's wrong with being a tourist attraction?" she asked. Fryberg's had done very well thanks to that tourist attraction. Over the years, what had been a small hobby shop had become a cottage industry unto itself with the entire town embracing the Bavarian atmosphere. "You saw our balance sheet. Those tourists are contributing a very healthy portion of our revenue."

"I also saw that the biggest growth came from your online store. In fact, while it's true retail sales have remained constant, your electronic sales have risen over fifteen percent annually."

And were poised to take another leap this year. Noelle had heard the projections. E-retail was the wave of the future. Brick-and-mortar stores like Fryberg's would soon be obsolete.

"Don't get me wrong. I think your late husband did a fantastic job of capitalizing on people's nostalgia," he said to Belinda.

Noelle's mother-in-law smiled. She always smiled when speaking about her late husband. "Ned used to say that Christmas was a universal experience."

"Hammond's has certainly done well by it."

Well? Hammond's had their entire business on the holiday, as had Fryberg's. *Nothing Says Christmas Like Hammond's Toys.* The company motto, repeated at the end of every ad, sung in Noelle's head.

"That's because everyone loves Christmas," she replied.

"Hmm." From the lack of enthusiasm in his response, she might as well have been talking about weather patterns. Then again, his emotional range didn't seem to go beyond brusque and chilly, so maybe that was enthusiastic for him.

"I don't care if they love the holiday or not. It's their shopping patterns I'm interested in, and from the data I've been seeing, more and more people are doing part, if not most of their shopping over the internet. The retailers who survive will be the ones who shift their business models accordingly. I intend to make sure Hammond's is one of those businesses."

"Hammond's," Noelle couldn't help noting. "Not Fryberg's."

"I'm hoping that by the end of the day, the two

stores will be on the way to becoming one and the same," he said.

"Wiping out sixty-five years of tradition just like that, are you?"

"Like I said, to survive, sometimes you have to embrace change."

Except they weren't embracing anything. Fryberg's was being swallowed up and dismantled so that Hammond's could change.

"I think what my daughter-in-law is trying to say is that the Fryberg name carries a great deal of value round these parts," said Belinda. "People are very loyal to my late husband and what he worked to create here."

"Loyalty's a rare commodity these days. Especially in the business world."

"It certainly is. Ned, my husband, had a way of inspiring it."

"Impressive," Hammond replied.

"It's because the Frybergs—Ned and Belinda— have always believed in treating their employees like family," Noelle told him. "And they were always on-site, visible to everyone." Although things had changed over the last few years as Belinda had been spending more and more time in Palm Beach. "I'm not sure working for a faceless CEO in Boston will engender the same feelings."

"What do you expect me to do? Move my office here?"

He looked at her. His gaze, sharp and direct, didn't so much look through a person as cut into them. The flecks of brown in his irises darkened, transforming what had been soft hazel. Self-consciousness curled through Noelle's midsection. She folded her arms tighter to keep the reaction from spreading.

"No. Just keep Fryberg's as a separate entity," she replied.

His brows lifted. "Really? You want me to keep one store separate when all the other properties under our umbrella carry the name Hammond?"

"Why not?" Noelle's palms started to sweat. She was definitely overstepping her authority right now. Belinda had already accepted Hammond's offer. Today's meeting was a friendly dialogue between an outgoing owner and the new CEO, to ensure a successful transition. She couldn't help it. With Belinda stepping down, someone had to protect what Ned had created. James Hammond certainly wasn't. To hear him, Fryberg's Christmas Castle was one step ahead of landlines in terms of obsolescence. She gave him two years tops before he decided "Hammond's" Christmas Castle didn't fit the corporate brand and started downsizing in the name of change. Bet he wouldn't blink an eye doing it either.

Oh, but she really, really, *really* disliked him. Thank goodness the corporate headquarters were in Boston. With luck, he'd go home after this visit and she'd never have to deal with him again.

"Our name recognition and reputation are important elements to our success," she continued. "All those people who line up to see Hammond's displays every Christmas? Would they still remember to make the pilgrimage if Hammond's suddenly became Jones's Toys?"

He chuckled. "Hammond's is hardly the same as Jones."

"Around here it might as well be."

"She makes an interesting point," Belinda said. Noelle felt her mother-in-law's sideways gaze. When it came to giving a pointed look, Belinda

Fryberg held her own. In fact, she could probably do it better than most since she always tossed in a dose of maternal reproach. "While you may think our physical store has a limited future, there's no need to hasten its demise prematurely. Maybe it would make more sense for Fryberg's to continue operating under its own name, at least for now."

Leaning back in his chair, Hammond steepled his fingertips together and tapped them against his lips. "I'm not averse to discussing the idea," he said finally.

I'm not averse... How big of him. Noelle bit her tongue.

Her mother-in-law, meanwhile, folded her hands and smiled. "Then why don't we do just that over lunch? I made reservations at the Nutcracker Inn downtown."

"I don't usually have lunch…"

No surprise there. Noelle had read once that sharks only ate every few days.

"Perhaps you don't," Belinda replied, "but for a woman my age, skipping meals isn't the best idea. Besides, I find business always goes smoother when accompanied by a bowl of gingerbread soup. You haven't lived until you've tried it."

Either Hammond's cheek muscles twitched at the word *gingerbread* or else they weren't used to smiling. "Very well," he said. "I have some calls to make first though. Why don't I meet you at the elevator in, say, fifteen minutes?"

"I'll see you there."

Returning Belinda's nod, he unfolded his lanky self from the chair and strode from the room. If only he'd keep walking, Noelle thought as she watched his back slip through the door. Keep walking all the way back to Boston.

"Well, that was a surprise." Belinda spoke the second the door shut behind him. "I hadn't realized you'd joined the mergers and acquisitions team."

"I'm sorry," Noelle replied. "But the way he was talking...it sounded like he planned to wipe Fryberg's off the map."

"You know I would never allow that."

She hung her head. "I know, and I'm sorry. On the plus side, he did say he would consider keeping the Fryberg's name."

"Even so, you can't keep getting angry every time he says something that rubs you the wrong way. This is Hammond's company now. You're going to have to learn to bite your tongue."

She'd better hope Noelle's tongue was thick enough to survive the visit then, because there was going to be a lot of biting.

"I just…" Starting now. Gritting her teeth, she turned and looked out the window. Below her, a school tour was lining up in front of the reindeer petting zoo, the same as they did every year, the Wednesday before Thanksgiving. Later on, they would make wish lists for their parents and trek over to the Candy Cane Forest to meet Santa Claus.

Her attention zeroed in on a little girl wearing a grimy pink snow jacket, the dirt visible from yards away, and she smiled nostalgically at the girl's obvious excitement. That excitement was what people like James Hammond didn't understand. Fryberg's was so much more than a toy store or tourist attraction. When you passed through that nutcracker-flanked gate, you entered a different world. A place where, for a few hours, little girls in charity bin hand-me-downs could trade their loneliness and stark reality for a little Christmas magic.

A warm hand settled on her shoulder. "I wish things could stay the same too," Belinda said, "but time marches on no matter how hard we try to stop it. Ned's gone, Kevin's gone, and I just don't have the energy to run this place by myself anymore.

"Besides, a chain like Hammond's can invest capital in this place that I don't have."

Capital, sure, but what about heart? Compassion was part of the Fryberg DNA. Noelle still remembered that day in sixth grade when Kevin invited her to his house and she felt the family's infectious warmth for the very first time.

"I don't fault you for wanting to retire," she said, leaning ever so slightly into the older woman's touch. "I just wish you hadn't sold to such a Grinch."

"He is serious, isn't he?" Belinda chuckled. "Must be all that dour Yankee heritage."

"Dour? Try frozen. The guy has about as much Christmas spirit as a block of ice."

Her mother-in-law squeezed her shoulder. "Fortunately for us, you have enough Christmas spirit for a dozen people. You'll keep the spirit alive. Unless you decide to move on, that is."

Noelle tried for tongue biting again and failed. They'd had this conversation before. It was another one of the reasons Belinda sold the business instead of simply retiring. She insisted Noelle not be tied down by the family business. A reason Noelle found utterly silly.

"You know I have zero intention of ever leaving Fryberg," she said.

"Oh, I know you think that now. But you're young. You're smart. There's an entire world out there beyond Fryberg's Toys."

Noelle shook her head. Not for her there wasn't. The store was too big a part of her.

It was all of her, really.

Her mother-in-law squeezed her shoulder again. "Kevin and Ned wouldn't want you to shortchange your future any more than I do."

At the mention of her late husband's wishes, Noelle bit back a familiar swell of guilt.

"Besides," Belinda continued, heading toward

her desk. "Who knows? Maybe you'll impress Mr. Hammond so much, he'll promote you up the corporate ladder."

"Him firing me is more likely," Noelle replied. She recalled how sharp Hammond's gaze had become when she dared to challenge him. Oh, yeah, she could picture him promoting her, all right.

"You never know" was all Belinda said. "I better go get ready for lunch. Don't want to keep our Mr. Hammond waiting. Are you joining us?"

And continue bonding with Mr. Hammond over a bowl of gingerbread soup? Thanks, but no thanks. "I think Mr. Hammond and I have had enough contact for the day. Better I save my tongue and let you and Todd fill me in on the visit later."

"That reminds me. On your way out, can you stop by Todd's office and let his secretary know that if he calls in after the funeral, I'd like to talk with him?"

"Sure thing."

Her answer was buried by the sound of the phone ringing.

"Oh, dear," Belinda said upon answering. "This

is Dick Greenwood. I'd better take it. Hopefully, he won't chat my ear off. Will you do me another favor and give Mr. Hammond a tour of the floor while I'm tied up?"

So much for being done with the man. "Of course." She'd donate a kidney if Belinda asked.

"And be nice."

"Yes, ma'am."

The kidney would have been easier.

"You're not going to have an insubordination problem, are you?"

On the other end of the line, Jackson Hammond's voice sounded far away. James might have blamed the overseas connection except he knew better. Jackson Hammond always sounded distant.

Struggling to keep the phone tucked under his ear, he reached for the paper towels. "Problem?" he repeated. "Hardly."

With her short black hair and red sweater dress, Noelle Fryberg was more of an attack elf. Too small and precious to do any real damage.

"Only reason she was in the meeting was because the new general manager had to attend a funeral, and she's the assistant GM." And because she was family. Apparently, the concept mattered to some people.

He shrugged and tossed his wadded towel into the basket. "Her objections were more entertaining than anything."

He'd already come to the same conclusion regarding the Fryberg name, but it was fun seeing her try to stare him into capitulation. She had very large, very soulful eyes. Her glaring at him was like being glared at by a kitten. He had to admire the effort though. It was more than a lot of—hell, most—people.

"All in all, the transition is going smooth as silk. I'm going to tour the warehouse this afternoon." And then hightail it back to the airstrip as soon as possible. With any luck, he'd be in Boston by eight that evening. Noelle Fryberg's verve might be entertaining, but not so much that he wanted to stick around Christmas Land a moment longer than necessary.

"Christmas is only four weeks away. You're

going to need that distribution center linked into ours as soon as possible."

"It'll get done," James replied. The reassurance was automatic. James learned a long time ago that his father preferred his world run as smoothly as possible. Complications and problems were things you dealt with on your own.

"If you need anything from my end, talk with Carli. I've asked her to be my point person while I'm in Vienna."

"Thank you." But James wouldn't need anything from his father's end. He'd been running the corporation for several years now while his father concentrated on overseas and other pet projects—like his new protégé, Carli, for example.

Then again, he hadn't needed his father since his parents' divorce. About the time his father made it clear he didn't want James underfoot. Not wanting their eldest son around was the one thing Jackson Hammond and his ex-wife had in common.

"How is the trip going?" James asked, turning to other, less bitter topics.

"Well enough. I'm meeting with Herr Burns in

the morning…" There was a muffled sound in the background. "Someone's knocking at the door. I have to go. We'll talk tomorrow, when you're back in the office."

The line disconnected before James had a chance to remind him tomorrow was Thanksgiving. Not that it mattered. He'd still be in the office.

He was always in the office. Wasn't like he had a family.

Belinda was nowhere in sight when James stepped into the hallway. Instead, he found the daughter-in-law waiting by the elevator, arms again hugging her chest. "Belinda had to take a call with Dick Greenwood," she told him.

"I'm sorry" was his automatic reply. Greenwood was a great vendor, but he was notorious for his chattiness. James made a point of avoiding direct conversations if he could.

Apparently, the daughter-in-law knew what he meant, because the corners of her mouth twitched. About as close to a smile as he'd seen out of her. "She said she'll join you as soon as she can. In the meantime, she thought you'd like a tour of the retail store."

"She did, did she?" More likely, she thought it would distract him while she was stuck on the phone.

Noelle shrugged. "She thought it would give you an idea of the foot traffic we handle on a day-to-day basis."

He'd seen the sales reports; he knew what kind of traffic they handled. Still, it couldn't hurt to check out the store. Hammond's was always on the lookout for new ways to engage their customers. "Are you going to be my guide?" he asked, reaching across to hit the elevator button.

"Yes, I am." If she thought he missed the soft sigh she let out before speaking, she was mistaken.

All the more reason to take the tour.

The doors opened, and James motioned for her to step in first. Partly to be a gentleman, but mostly because holding back gave him an opportunity to steal a surreptitious look at her figure. The woman might be tiny, but she was perfectly proportioned. Make that normally proportioned, he amended. Too many of the women he met had try-hard figures. Worked out and enhanced to artificial perfection. Noelle looked fit, but she still carried a little more below than she did on top, which he appreciated.

"We bill ourselves as the country's largest toy store," Noelle said once the elevator doors shut. "The claim is based on square footage. We are the largest retail space in the continental US. This weekend alone we'll attract thousands of customers."

"Black Friday weekend. The retailers' best friend," he replied. Then, because he couldn't resist poking the bee's nest a little, he added, "That is, until Cyber Monday came along. These days we move almost as much inventory online. Pretty soon people won't come out for Black Friday at all. They'll do their shopping Thanksgiving afternoon while watching TV."

"Hammond's customers might, but you can't visit a Christmas wonderland via a computer."

That again. He turned to look at her. "Do you really think kids five or six years from now are going to care about visiting Santa Claus?"

"Of course they are. It's Santa."

"I hate to break it to you, but kids are a little more realistic these days. They grow fast. Our greeting card fantasy holiday is going to get harder and harder to sell."

"Especially if you insist on calling it a fantasy."

What should he call it? Fact? "Belinda wasn't kidding when she said you were loyal, was she?"

"The Frybergs are family. Of course I would be loyal."

Not necessarily, but James didn't feel like arguing the point.

"Even if I weren't—related that is—I'd respect what Ned and Belinda created." She crossed her arms. Again. "They understood that retail is about more than moving inventory."

Her implication was clear: she considered him a corporate autocrat who was concerned solely with the bottom line. While she might be correct, he didn't intend to let her get away with the comment unchallenged.

Mirroring her posture, he tilted his head and looked straight at her. "Is that so? What exactly is it about then?"

"People, of course."

"Of course." She was not only loyal, but naive. Retail was *all* about moving product. All the fancy window dressing she specialized in was to convince people to buy the latest and greatest, and then to buy the next latest and greatest the following year. And so on and so forth.

At that moment, the elevator opened and before them lay Fryberg's Toys in all its glory. Aisle upon aisle of toys, spread out like a multicolored promised land. There were giant stuffed animals arranged by environment, lions and tigers in the jungle, cows and horses by the farm. Construction toys were spread around a jobsite, around which cars zipped on a multilevel racetrack. There was even a wall of televisions blasting the latest video games. A special display for every interest, each one overflowing with products for sale.

"Oh, yeah," he murmured, "it's totally about the people."

A remote-control drone zipped past their heads as they walked toward the center aisle. A giant teddy bear made of plastic building bricks marked the entrance like the Colossus of Rhodes.

"It's like Christmas morning on steroids," he remarked as they passed under the bear's legs.

"This is the Christmas Castle, after all. Everything should look larger-than-life and magical. To stir the imagination."

Not to mention the desire for plastic bricks and stuffed animals, thought James.

"Santa's workshop and the Candy Cane Forest are located at the rear of the building," she said pointing to an archway bedecked with painted holly and poinsettia. "That's also where Ned's model train layout is located. It used to be a much larger section, but now it's limited to one room-size museum."

Yet something else lost to the march of time, James refrained from saying. The atmosphere was chilly enough. Looking around he noticed their aisle led straight toward the archway, and that the only way to avoid Santa was to go to the end, turn and head back up a different aisle.

He nodded at the arch. "What's on the other side?" he asked.

"Other side of what?"

"Santa's woods or whatever it is."

"Santa's workshop and Candy Cane Forest," she corrected. "There's a door that leads back into the store, or they can continue on to see the reindeer."

"Meaning they go home to purchase their child's wish item online from who-knows-what site."

"Or come back another day. Most people don't do their Christmas shopping with the kids in tow."

"How about in April, when they aren't Christmas shopping? They walk outside to see the reindeer and poof! There goes your potential sale."

That wouldn't do at all. "After the kids visit Santa, the traffic should be rerouted back into the store so the parents can buy whatever it is Little Susie or Johnny wished for."

"You want to close off access to the reindeer?"

She needn't look so horrified. It wasn't as though he'd suggested euthanizing the creatures. "I want customers to buy toys. And they aren't going to if they are busy looking at reindeer. What's that?"

He pointed to a giant Moose-like creature wearing a Santa's hat and wreath standing to the right of the archway. It took up most of the wall space, forcing the crowd to congregate toward the middle. As a result, customers looking to walk past the archway to another aisle had to battle a throng of children.

"Oh, that's Fryer Elk, the store mascot," Noelle replied. "Ned created him when he opened the store. Back in the day, he appeared in the ads. They retired him in the eighties and he's been here ever since."

"He's blocking the flow of traffic. He should be somewhere else."

For a third time, James got the folded arm treatment. "He's an institution," she replied, as if that was reason enough for his existence.

He could be Ned Fryberg standing there stuffed himself, and he would still be hindering traffic. Letting out a long breath, James reached into his breast pocket for his notebook. Once the sale was finalized, he would send his operations manager out here to evaluate the layout.

"You really don't have any respect for tradition, do you?" Noelle asked.

He peered over his pen at her. Just figuring this out, was she? That's what happened when you spent a fortune crafting a corporate image. People started believing the image was real.

"No," he replied. "I don't. In fact…" He put his notebook away. "We might as well get something straight right now. As far as I'm concerned, the only thing that matters is making sure Hammond's stays profitable for the next fifty years. Everything else can go to blazes."

"Everything," she repeated. Her eyes narrowed.

"Everything, and that includes elks, tradition and especially Chris—"

He never got a chance to finish.

CHAPTER TWO

FOUR STITCHES AND a concussion. That's what the emergency room doctor told Noelle. "He's fortunate. Those props can do far worse," she added. "Your associates really shouldn't be flying remote-control drones inside."

"So they've been told," Noelle replied. In no uncertain terms by James Hammond once he could speak.

The drone had slammed into the back of his head, knocking him face-first into a pile of model racecar kits. The sight of the man sprawled on the floor might have been funny if not for the blood running down the back of his skull. Until that minute, she'd been annoyed as hell at the man for his obvious lack of respect toward Fryberg tradition. Seeing the blood darkening his hair quickly checked her annoyance. As blood was wont to do. That was until she turned him over and he started snarling about careless associates and customer safety. Then she went back to being annoyed. Only this time, it was because the man had a point. What if the drone had struck a customer—a child? Things could have been even worse. As it was, half of Miss Speroni's first grade class was probably going to have nightmares from witnessing the accident.

Then there was the damage to James Hammond himself. Much as she disliked the man, stitches and a concussion were nothing to sneeze at.

"How long before he's ready for discharge?" she asked.

"My nurse is bandaging the stitches right now," the doctor replied. "Soon as I get his paperwork written up, he'll be all yours."

Oh, goodie. Noelle didn't realize she'd gotten custody. She went back to the waiting room where Belinda was finishing up a phone call.

"Bob is working on a statement for the press," her mother-in-law told her. "And we're pulling the product off the shelves per advice from the lawyers. Thankfully, the incident didn't get caught on camera so we won't have to deal with that. I doubt Mr. Hammond would like being a social media sensation."

"I'm not sure Mr. Hammond likes much of anything," Noelle replied. She was thinking of the remark he made right before the drone struck him. "Did you know, he actually said he doesn't like Christmas? How can the man think that and run a store like Hammond's?" Or Fryberg's.

"Obviously, his disdain hasn't stopped him from doubling Hammond's profits over the past two years," Belinda replied. "What matters isn't that he like Christmas, but that he keeps the people in Fryberg employed, which he will."

"Hope they like working for Mr. Frosty. Did you know he wants to get rid of Fryer?"

"Well, some change is bound to happen," Belinda said.

"I know," Noelle grumbled. She bowed her head. She really did. Same way she understood that the retail industry was changing. She also knew she was acting irrational and childish about the entire situation. Ever since Belinda announced the sale, however, she'd been unable to catch her breath. It felt like there were fingers clawing inside her looking for purchase. A continual churning sensation. Like she was about to lose her grip.

James Hammond's arrival only made the feeling worse.

"Doesn't mean I have to like it though," she said referring to the prospect of change.

Belinda nudged her shoulder. "Sweetheart, you wouldn't be you if you did. Cheer up. Mr. Hammond will be out of your hair soon."

"Not soon enough," she replied.

"What wouldn't be soon enough?" Hammond's voice caused her to start in her chair. Turning, she saw a nurse pushing him toward her. He was slouched down in a wheelchair, a hand propping his head. Noelle caught a glimpse of a white bandage on the back of his scalp.

"The bandage can come off tomorrow," the nurse told them.

"How are you feeling, Mr. Hammond?" Belinda asked.

"Like someone split my head open. Who knew such a little device could pack such a wallop?"

"Lots of things pack a wallop when they're going thirty miles an hour. We pulled the toy from the shelves. Though I doubt it would have been popular anyway, once parents heard what happened."

"Don't blame them. Thing could slice an ear off." Groaning, he leaned forward and buried his face in both hands as though one was suddenly not enough to hold it up. "I'm going to have Hammond's pull them too as soon as I get back to Boston," he spoke through his fingers.

"That won't be anytime soon, I'm afraid. You heard what Dr. Nelson said," the nurse warned.

"What did she say?" Noelle asked. She didn't like the sound of the nurse's comment.

Hammond waved a hand before cradling his head again. "Nothing."

"Mr. Hammond has a slight concussion. He's been advised to rest for the next couple of days. That includes no air travel."

"You mean you're staying here?" No, no, no. Noelle's stomach started to twist. He was supposed to go away, not stick around for the weekend.

"The doctor merely recommended I rest," James replied. "No one said it was mandatory."

"Perhaps not, but it's generally a good idea to take doctors' advice," Belinda said.

"We're talking about a handful of stitches. Nothing I haven't had before. I'll be fine. Why don't we go have our lunch as planned and finish our conversation? I could use some food in my stomach. What kind of soup did you say they made?"

"Gingerbread," Noelle replied.

"The only place you should be going is to bed," the nurse said.

Much as Noelle hated to admit it, the nurse was right. He was looking paler by the minute. She remembered how unsteady he'd been right after the accident; he could barely sit up.

Funny, but he still looked formidable despite the pallor. A virile invalid. Noelle didn't think it possible. Must be the combination of square jaw and broad shoulders, she decided. And the dark suit. Black made everyone look intimidating.

Again, he waved off the nurse's advice. "Nonsense. I rested while waiting for the doctor. Why don't we go have our lunch as planned and finish our conversation? I could use some food in my stomach. What kind of soup did you say they made?"

"I just told you."

A crease deepened between his eyes. "You did?"

"Uh-huh. Two seconds ago."

"That only proves I'm hungry. I'm having trouble listening." He pushed himself to a standing position, squaring his shoulders proudly when he reached his feet. His upper body swayed back and forth unsteadily. "See?" he said. "Fine. Let's go."

Noelle looked over her shoulder at Belinda who shook her head in return. "I'm not going to negotiate anything while you're unsteady on your feet," her mother-in-law said. "I won't be accused of taking advantage when you're not thinking straight."

James laughed. "You're a smart businesswoman, Belinda, but I can assure you, no one ever takes advantage of me."

"That I can believe," Noelle murmured.

He looked at her and smiled. "I'll take that as a compliment, Mrs. Fryberg. Now how about we go get that lunch we missed…"

It took two steps for him to lose his balance. His eyes started to roll back in his head, and his knees started to buckle.

Noelle reached him first. "Okay, that's enough," she said, reaching around his waist. Thanks to the size difference, it took a minute to maneuver him, but eventually she managed to lower him into the wheelchair. Unfortunately, the downward momentum pulled her along as well. She landed with one hand pressed against his torso and knee wedged between his thighs. Man, but he was solid. A tall, lean block of granite.

She looked up to find herself nose to nose with him. Up close, his eyes were far more dappled than she realized, the green more of an accent color than true eye shade.

He had freckles too. A smattering across the bridge of his nose.

Cold-blooded businessmen weren't supposed to have freckles.

"Think you might listen to the nurse now?" she asked.

"I was lightheaded for a moment, that's all."

"Lightheaded, huh?" She pushed herself to her

feet. To her embarrassment, the move required splaying her hand wider, so that the palm of her hand pressed over his heart. Fortunately, he was too dizzy or distracted to comment.

"Any more lightheaded and you would have hit the floor," she told him. "Are you trying to get more stitches?"

"I'm not…"

"Face it, Mr. Hammond, you're in no condition to do anything but rest," Belinda said. "We'll talk when you're feeling better. Monday."

"Monday?" He'd started to rest his head in his hands again, but when Belinda spoke, he jerked his head upward. The pain crossing his face made Noelle wince. "Why wait until then? I won't need that many days to recover."

"Maybe not, but that is the next time I'll be able to see you. Tomorrow is Thanksgiving. The only business I'll be discussing is whether the stuffing is too dry."

"What about Friday?"

Noelle answered for her. "Black Friday, remember? Around these parts, it's the kickoff for the annual Christmas festival, the biggest weekend of our year."

"I'll be much too busy to give you the proper time," Belinda added.

Noelle watched the muscle twitching in Hammond's jaw. Clearly, he preferred being the one who dictated the schedule, and not the other way around.

"Let me get this straight." Whether his voice was low by design or discomfort, Noelle couldn't guess. His tension came though nevertheless. "I'm not allowed to fly home for the next twenty-four hours…"

"At least," the nurse said.

The muscle twitched again. "*At least* twenty-four hours," he corrected. "Nor will you meet with me for the next five days?"

"That's correct," Belinda replied. "We can meet first thing Monday morning, and conclude our preliminary negotiations."

"I see." He nodded. Slowly. Anyone with two eyes could tell he didn't appreciate this change in plans at all. Noelle would be lying if she didn't say it gave her a tiny trill of satisfaction. Payback for his wanting to toss Fryer.

"Fine," he said, leaning back in his chair. "We'll talk Monday. Only because my head hurts too much to argue." Noelle had a feeling he wasn't kidding. "What was the name of that hotel?"

"The Nutcracker Inn," she replied.

"Right, that one. I'm going to need a room, and something to eat. What did you say that soup was?"

"Gingerbread." It was the third time he'd asked. She looked at the nurse who nodded.

"Temporary short-term memory loss can happen with concussions. It should recede soon enough. However, I think you might have a more pressing problem."

"I do?"

"He does?"

The two of them spoke at the same time. "I'm not sure the Nutcracker has any rooms," the nurse replied. "You know how booked it gets during the holidays."

"Wait a second." James tried to look up at the

nurse, only to wince and close his eyes. "Please don't tell me there's no room at the inn."

"Wouldn't be the first time," the nurse replied. "Did you know that once we even had a baby born—"

"I doubt Mr. Hammond will have to do anything quite as dramatic," Noelle interjected. No need for the conversation to head down that particular road.

The nurse offered a tight-lipped smile. Apparently, she didn't appreciate being cut off. "Either way, you're going to need someone to look in on you. Doctor's orders."

"The concierge will love that request," Hammond muttered.

"We could arrange for a private duty nurse."

"Good grief," Belinda said. "That doesn't sound pleasant at all."

"Pleasant isn't exactly on the table right now." Hammond's eyes had grown heavy lidded and his words were slurred. It was obvious the entire conversation was exhausting him, and Noelle couldn't help but feel bad.

Although she doubted he'd appreciate the compassion. A man like Hammond, with his disregard for sentiment and tradition, would despise showing any hint of vulnerability.

"Of course pleasant is on the table," Belinda said. "This is Fryberg." The meaning behind her emphasis was obvious.

Hammond let out a low groan. Still feeling compassionate, Noelle decided the noise was coincidental.

Her mother-in-law continued as if the noise never happened. "We're not going to let you spend your weekend in some hotel room, eating room service and being attended to by a stranger. You'll spend the weekend with me. That way you can recuperate, and enjoy a proper Thanksgiving as well."

The strangest look crossed Hammond's face. Part surprise, part darkness as though her mother-in-law's suggestion unnerved him. Noelle didn't picture him as a man who got unnerved. Ever.

"I don't want to put you out," he said.

"You won't. I have plenty of room. I'll even make you some…oh, shoot." A look crossed her features, not nearly as dark as Hammond's, but definitely distressed.

"What is it?" Noelle asked.

"The Orion House Dinner is this evening. I completely forgot."

In all the craziness, so had Noelle. Fryberg's was being honored for its fund-raising efforts on behalf of homeless veterans. "Would you mind?" her mother-in-law asked. "I don't want Orion House to think I don't appreciate the honor. The project meant so much to Ned."

"I know," replied Noelle. After Kevin's death, her father-in-law had channeled his grief into helping as many veteran programs as possible. Orion House had topped the list. "He was very passionate about wanting to help."

"That he was," Belinda said, getting the far-away look she always got when they discussed Ned. The family had been through a lot these past years, and yet they continued to channel their energy into the community. Their dedication in the face of grief made her proud to bear the Fryberg name.

"Would you mind stepping in instead?"

"Not at all," she told her. "I'd love to." It'd be an honor to accept an award for them.

"Thank goodness." The older woman let out a long sigh. "I was afraid that because of our words earlier... Never mind." Whatever her mother-in-law had been about to say she waved away. "Let me pull my car around. I'll help you get Mr. Hammond settled, and then go home to change."

Help her...? Wait... What exactly had she agreed to do?

Noelle opened her mouth, closed it, then opened it again. Nothing came out though. That's because she knew what she'd agreed to. As surely as the sickening feeling growing in her stomach.

Somehow, James Hammond had become *her* responsibility. She looked over to her mother-in-law, but Belinda was busy fishing through her purse. And here she thought she would be free of the man. Talk about your sick karmic jokes. If only she'd been the one hit in the head.

"Do you need an extra copy of the discharge instructions?" the nurse asked her.

"No," Noelle replied with a sigh. "I know what to expect."

There was only one consolation, if you could call it that. Hammond looked about as thrilled over this change of events as she was.

Goodie. They could be miserable together.

A few minutes later, James found himself being wheeled outside behind a tiny bundle of annoyance, who marched toward the waiting sedan with her arms yet again wrapped tightly across her chest. A voice behind his headache wondered if they were permanently attached to her body that way.

"Why don't you take the front seat?" Belinda opened the passenger door. "I've pulled it all the way back so you'll have plenty of leg room."

Front seat, back seat. Didn't make much difference. Neither were the cockpit of his private plane. His head felt split in two, the world was tipping on its axis and he wanted nothing more than to be in his bed back in Boston. Damn drone.

He pushed himself to his feet only to have the world rock back and forth like a seesaw. A second later, an arm wrapped around his biceps, steadying him, and he smelled the sweet scent of orange blossoms. The elf. He recognized the perfume from the confines of the elevator. Funny, but he expected her to smell Christmassy, not like Florida sunshine. Maybe they were out of sugar cookie perfume this week.

"Something wrong?"

Turning his head—barely—he saw her frowning at him and realized he'd snorted out loud at his joke. "Do you really need to ask?"

He was being an ass, he knew that, but with stitches in his scalp, surely he was entitled to a little churlishness?

The frown deepened. "Watch your head," she replied.

James did as he was told, and as his reward, the orange blossoms—as well as her grip—disappeared. In their absence, his headache intensified. He found himself slumped against a leather armrest with his fingers pressed against his temple to hold his head up.

"Fortunately, we don't have to drive too far," he heard Belinda say. "Noelle only lives a short distance from town."

"Great." What he really wanted to say was that

two feet was too far what with the lights outside dipping and rocking as they passed by. Thankfully the sun had set. If those were buildings bobbing, he'd be lurching the contents of his stomach all over his Bostonians. He closed his eyes, and did his best to imagine orange blossoms.

"The nurse seemed to think the worst of the dizziness would pass by tomorrow," Noelle said from behind him.

"Thank God," he whispered. If true, then maybe he could snag a ride to the airport and fly home, doctor's orders be damned. He bet the elf would drive him. After all, she didn't want him at her house any more than he wanted to be there. He'd caught the look on the woman's face when Belinda foisted him on her.

Foisted. What a perfect word for the situation. Stuck where he didn't want to be, dependent on people who didn't want him around.

Story of his life.

Great. He'd moved from churlish to pity party. Why not round out the trifecta and start whining too?

How he hated this. Hated having no choice.

Hated being weak and needy. He hadn't needed anyone since he was twelve years old. Needing and foisting were incompatible concepts.

"It's too bad you can't look out the window," Belinda said. "The town looks beautiful all lit up."

James pried open one eye to see building after building decorated with Christmas lights. *Ugh*. One in particular had a giant evergreen dripping with red and green.

"That's the Nutcracker Inn. The Bavarian market is next door. It'll be packed on Friday for the festival."

"I doubt Mr. Hammond is very interested in a tour, Belinda."

"I'm merely pointing out a few of the landmarks since he's going to be here all weekend."

Not if he could help it, thought James.

"The man can't remember what kind of soup they serve—I doubt he'll remember what the place looks like."

"There's no need to be harsh, Noelle Fryberg."

"Yes, ma'am."

Actually, James rather liked the harshness. Beat

being treated like a patient. "Pumpkin," he replied.

"Excuse me?" Belinda asked.

"The soup. It's pumpkin."

"You mean gingerbread," Noelle replied.

"Oh. Right." He knew it was some kind of seasonal flavor. His cheeks grew warm.

Belinda patted him on the knee. "Don't worry about it, Mr. Hammond. I'm sure you'll be back to normal by tomorrow."

"Let's hope so," he heard the elf mutter.

James couldn't have agreed with her more.

CHAPTER THREE

THE NEXT MORNING James woke to what had to be the best-smelling candle in the universe—sweet with traces of allspice and cinnamon—which was odd since he didn't normally buy candles. Maybe the smell had something to do with the stinging sensation on the back of his head and the vague memories of dark hair and kitten eyes dancing on the edge of his brain.

And orange blossoms. For some reason, the first thought in his mind was that as delicious as the candle smelled, it wasn't orange blossoms.

Slowly, he pried open an eye. What the…?

This wasn't his Back Bay condo. He sprang up, only to have a sharp pain push him back down on the bed.

Sofa, he amended. He was lying facedown on a leather sofa, his cheek swallowed by a large memory foam pillow. Gingerly, he felt the back of his skull, his fingers meeting a patch of gauze and tape.

The drone. This must be Noelle Fryberg's living room. Last thing he remembered was leaning into her warm body as she led him through the front door. Explained why he had orange blossoms on the brain. The memory of the smell eased the tension between his shoulder blades.

Once the vertigo abated, he surveyed his surroundings. Given her slavish devotion to Fryberg's vision, he pictured his hostess living in a mirror image of the Christmas Castle, with baskets of sugarplums and boughs of holly. He'd been close. The house definitely had the same stucco and wood architecture as the rest of the town, although she'd thankfully forgone any year-round Christmas motif. Instead, the inside was pleasantly furnished with simple, sturdy furniture like the large pine cabinet lining the wall across the way. Brightly colored plates hung on the wall behind it. Homey. Rustic. With not a chandelier or trace of Italian marble to be found.

"You're awake."

A pair of shapely legs suddenly appeared in his

line of vision, followed seconds later by a pair of big cornflower-colored eyes as the elf squatted down by his head. "I was coming in to check on you. I'm supposed to make sure you don't fall into a coma while sleeping," she said.

"I haven't."

"Obviously."

As obvious as her joy over having to play nurse-maid.

She looked less elfish than yesterday. More girl next door. The red dress had been shucked in favor of a white-and-red University of Wisconsin sweatshirt and jeans, and her short hair was pulled away from her face with a bright red head-band. James didn't think it was possible to pull back short hair, but she had. It made her eyes look like one of those paintings from the seventies. The ones where everyone had giant sad eyes. Only in this case, they weren't sad; they were antipathetic.

He tried sitting up again. Slowly this time, making sure to keep his head and neck as still as possible. He felt like an awkward idiot. How was it that people in movies bounced back from head wounds in minutes? Here he was sliding his legs to the floor like he was stepping onto ice.

"How did I end up here?" he asked.

Her mouth turned downward. "Do you mean the house or the sofa?"

"The sofa."

"Good. For a minute I was afraid you didn't remember anything." She stood up, taking her blue eyes from his vision unless he looked up, which didn't feel like the best idea. "You collapsed on it soon as we got through the door last night," she told him. "I tried to convince you to go upstairs to the bedroom, but you refused to budge."

That sounded vaguely familiar. "Stairs were too much work."

"That's what you said last night. Anyway, since you refused to move from the sofa, I gave you a pillow, threw an afghan over you and called it a night."

Out of the corner of his eye, James saw a flash of bright blue yarn piled on the floor near his feet. Tightness gripped his chest at the notion of someone tucking a blanket around his legs while he slept. Cradling his head while they placed a pillow underneath.

"Wait a second," he said as a realization struck him. "You checked on me every few hours?"

"I had to. Doctor's orders."

"What about sleep? Did you…"

"Don't worry—I didn't put myself out any more than necessary."

But more than she preferred. He was but an unwanted responsibility after all. The tightness eased, and the familiar numbness returned. "I'm glad. I'd hate to think you had to sacrifice too much."

"Bare minimum, I assure you. Belinda would have my head if you died on my watch. In case you hadn't guessed, she takes her responsibility to others very seriously. Especially those injured in her store."

His store now. James let the slip pass uncommented. "Good policy. I'm sure your lawyers appreciate the extra effort."

"It's not policy," she quickly shot back. Her eyes simmered with contention. "It's compassion. The Frybergs have always believed in taking care of others. Belinda especially. I'll have you know that I've seen her literally give a stranger the coat off her back."

"I apologize," James replied. "I didn't mean to insinuate…"

She held up her hand. "Whatever. Just know that lawsuits are the last thing on Belinda's mind.

"You have no idea how special the Fryberg family is," she continued. Driving home the point. "Ned and Belinda were…are…the best people you'll ever meet. The whole town loves them."

"Duly noted," James replied. Must be nice, having a family member care so much they sprang to your defense at the slightest ill word. "I'll watch my language from now on."

"Thank you."

"You're welcome."

They both fell silent. James sat back on the sofa and rubbed his neck, an uncomfortable itch having suddenly danced across his collar. Normally silence didn't bother him; he didn't know why this lapse in conversation felt so awkward.

Probably because the entire situation was awkward. If they were in Boston, he would be the host. He would be offering to whip up a cappuccino and his signature scrambled eggs, the way he did for all his overnight guests. Instead, he was sitting on her sofa, feeling very much like the obligation that he was.

And here he'd thought he was done feeling that way ever again.

Noelle broke the silence first. Tugging on her sweatshirt the way an officer might tug on his jacket, she cleared her throat. "I'm heading back into the kitchen. You might as well go back to sleep. It's still early. Not even seven-thirty."

"You're awake."

"I have cooking to do. You're supposed to rest."

"I'm rested out." Headache or not, his body was still on East Coast time, and according to it, he'd already slept several hours past his usual wake time. "I don't think I could sleep more if I wanted to."

"Suit yourself," she said with a shrug. "TV remote's on the end table if you want it. I'll be in the kitchen." The unspoken *Stay out of my way* came loud and clear.

She turned and padded out the door. Although

James had never been one to ogle women, he found himself watching her jean-clad rear end. Some women were born to wear jeans, and the elf was one of them. With every step, her hips swayed from side to side like a well-toned bell. It was too bad the woman disliked his presence; her attractiveness was one of the few positive things about this debacle of a trip.

He needed to go back to Boston. It was where he belonged. Where he was...well, if not wanted, at least comfortable.

Slowly, he pushed himself to his feet. The room spun a little, but not nearly as badly as it had yesterday, or even fifteen minutes earlier, for that matter. If he managed to walk to the kitchen without problem, he was leaving. Grant him and Noelle a reprieve.

Plans settled, he made his way to the kitchen. Happily, the room only spun a little. He found his hostess in the center of the room pulling a bright yellow apron over her head. The delicious aroma from before hung heavy in the air. It wasn't a candle at all, but some kind of pie. Pumpkin, he realized, taking a deep breath.

His stomach rumbled. "I don't suppose I could get a cup of coffee," he said when she turned around.

She pointed to the rear cupboard where a full pot sat on the coffee maker burner. "Cups are in the cupboard above. There's cereal and toast if you want any breakfast. Do you need me to pour?" she added belatedly.

"No, thank you. I can manage." He made his way over to the cupboard. Like everything else in the house, the mugs were simple, yet sturdy. He was beginning to think she was the only delicate-looking thing in the house. "You have a nice place," he remarked as he poured.

"You sound surprised."

"Do I?" he replied. "I don't mean to."

"In that case, thank you. Kevin and his father came up with the design."

That explained the resemblance to the Christmas Castle.

"I'm curious," he said, leaning against the counter. She had bent over to look in the oven, giving him another look at her bottom. "Is there some kind of rule that the houses all have to look..."

"Look like what?" she asked, standing up.

"Alike." Like they'd all been plucked off a picture postcard.

"Well the idea *is* to resemble a European village. That's part of what makes us such a popular tourist attraction."

She was tossing around his words from yesterday. He'd insulted her again.

Which he knew before asking the question. Hell, it was why he'd asked it. Their exchange earlier reminded him how much he'd enjoyed her backbone yesterday. Next to her cute figure, pushing her buttons was the only other thing that made this trip enjoyable. "I'm sure it does," he replied.

"What is that supposed to mean?"

James shrugged. "Nothing. I was simply noting the town had a distinctive theme is all, and wondered if it was by design. Now I know."

"I'm sure you already knew from your research," she said, folding her arms. She had the closed-off pose down to a science. "You just felt like mocking the town."

"Actually..." What could he say? He doubted

she'd enjoy knowing her anger entertained him. "Maybe I did."

She opened her mouth, and he waited for her to toss an insult in his direction. Instead she closed her lips again and spun around. Immediately, James regretted pushing too far. What did he expect? Surely, he knew she wouldn't find him as entertaining as he found her. Quite the opposite. She disliked him the same as everyone else. Pushing her buttons guaranteed the status quo.

There was one thing he could say that she might like.

"Your pie smells delicious, by the way. I'm sorry I won't get to taste it."

That got her attention. She turned back around. "Why not?"

Leaning against the counter, he took a long sip of his coffee. Damn, but she made a hearty cup. "Because as soon as I have my coffee and grab a shower, you're driving me to the airstrip so I can fly back to Boston."

Noelle almost dropped the pie she was taking out of the oven. Had she heard right? Not that she wouldn't be glad to see the back of him, but… "I thought the doctor said no flying."

"Doctors say a lot of things."

"Yeah, but in this case…" She flashed back to his falling into her at the hospital. "You could barely stand without getting dizzy."

"That was yesterday. Clearly, that's not the case today."

No, it wasn't. He appeared to be standing quite nicely against her counter, all wrinkled and fresh with sleep as he was.

The guy might be annoying, but he wore bed-head well.

Still, she couldn't believe he was serious about flying an airplane less than twenty-four hours after getting whacked in the head. What if he got dizzy again and crashed the plane? "It doesn't sound like the wisest of plans," she said.

From over his coffee mug, he looked at her with an arched brow. "You'd rather I stick around here with you all weekend?"

"No, but…"

"Then why do you care whether I fly home or not?"

Good question. Why did she care? She looked down at the golden-brown pie still in her hands. Setting it on the cooling rack, she took off her oven mitts, then nudged the oven door shut with her hip.

"I don't care," she said, turning back around. "I'm surprised is all. In my experience, doctors don't advise against things without reason.

"Why are you so eager to leave Fryberg anyway?" she asked. She could already guess the answer. It'd been clear from his arrival he didn't think much of their town.

Unless, that is, he had a different reason for returning to Boston. Something more personal. "If you have Thanksgiving plans with someone, wouldn't they prefer you play it safe?"

His coffee cup muffled the words, but she could swear he said "Hardly." It wasn't a word she'd expected him to use. *Hardly* was the same as saying *unlikely*, which couldn't be the case. A man as handsome as Hammond would have dozens of women interested in him. Just because he rubbed her the wrong way…

She must have misheard.

Still, it wasn't someone special calling him home. And she doubted it was because of Black Friday either. He could get sales reports via his phone; there was no need to physically be in Boston.

That left her original reason. "I'm sorry if our little town isn't comfortable enough for you to stick around."

"Did I say it wasn't comfortable?"

"You didn't have to," Noelle replied. "Your disdain has been obvious."

"As has yours," he shot back.

"I—"

"Let's face it, Mrs. Fryberg. You haven't exactly rolled out the welcome mat. Not that I mind," he said, taking a drink, "but let's not pretend the antipathy has been one-sided."

Maybe it wasn't, but he'd fired the first shot.

Noelle's coffee cup sat on the edge of the butcher-block island where she'd set it down earlier. Seeing the last quarter cup was ice-cold, she made her way to the coffee maker to top off the cup.

"What did you expect," she said, reaching past

him, "coming in here and announcing you were phasing out the Christmas Castle?"

"No, I said the castle was near the end of its lifespan. You're the one who got all overprotective and jumped to conclusions."

"Because you called it a fading tourist attraction."

"I said no such thing."

"Okay, maybe not out loud, but you were definitely thinking it."

"Was I, now?" he replied with a snort. "I didn't realize you were a mind reader."

"Oh, please, I could hear it in your voice. I don't have to be psychic to know you dislike the whole concept, even before you started making efficiency suggestions."

She set the pot back on the burner, so she could look him square in the eye. The two of them were wedged in the small spot, their shoulders abutting. "Or are you going to tell me that's not true?"

"No," he replied, in an even voice, "it's true. You shouldn't take it personally."

"Are you serious? Of course I'm going to take it personally. It's Fryberg's." The store represented everything good that had ever happened in her life since she was seven years old. "You didn't even want to keep the name!"

"I already conceded on that point, remember?"

"I remember." And considering how quickly he conceded, he'd probably already decided he didn't care. "That doesn't mitigate the other changes you want to make." The reindeer. Fryer. Those suggestions were the tip of the iceberg. Before anyone knew, her version of Fryberg's would be gone forever.

"Forgive me for wanting to improve the store's bottom line."

"Our bottom line is perfectly fine." As she glared into her coffee cup, she heard Hammond chuckle.

"So what you're saying is that you all would have been better off if I'd stayed in Boston."

"Exactly," she gritted.

"And you wonder why I don't want to stay in Fryberg."

Noelle's jaw muscles went slack. She looked back up in time to see Hammond tipping back the last of his drink. "I don't make a habit of staying where I'm not wanted," he said, setting the cup on the counter. "I'm certainly not about to start now. Would you mind if I grabbed that shower now? Then you can drop me off at the airstrip, and we'll both be free from an uncomfortable situation."

While he walked out of the kitchen, Noelle went back to contemplating the contents of her cup. She was waiting for a sense of relief to wash over her. After all, he was right; his leaving did free them both from an uncomfortable situation.

Why then wasn't she relieved?

Maybe because your behavior helped drive the man out of town? her conscience replied as she rubbed away a sudden chill from her right arm.

Perhaps she had been...prickly. Something about the man got under her skin. Everything he said felt like a direct assault on her life. Between the company being sold and Belinda moving to Florida, she felt cast adrift. Like a part of her had been cut away. The only things she had left were the castle, the town and its traditions. Without them, she'd go back to being...

Nothing. No, she'd be worse than nothing. She'd

be the nameless little girl whose mother left her in the stable. She'd rather be nothing.

Still, regardless of how angry Hammond made her, she still had a responsibility as a host. Belinda would have never been as argumentative and… well, as bratty…as she'd been.

She found Hammond in the living room folding last night's cover. As he bowed his head to match one corner to another, he wobbled slightly, clearly off-balance. A stab of guilt passed through her. No way was he better.

"You're going to have to keep your head dry," she said, taking one end of the afghan for him. After making sure the folds were straight enough, she walked her end toward him. "That glue the doctor used to cover your stitches needs to stay dry until tomorrow. I could draw you a bath though." They met in the center, their fingers tangling slightly as he passed her his end.

"Anything that gets me clean works fine. Thank you."

Hammond's index finger ran along the inside of hers as he spoke. Coincidence, but Noelle got a tingle anyway. It had been a long time since a

"There's blood on your collar," she said. It was the first thing that sprang to mind, and she needed something to explain her sudden loss of words. "Your shirt is ruined."

"Looks like the drone claims another victim." Hammond fingered the stiff corner. The red-brown stain covered most of the right side. "I'll toss it out when I get home. Who knew something so small could cause so much damage?"

"Consider yourself lucky it wasn't something bigger," Noelle replied. Her senses regained, she continued toward the linen closet. "Could have been a remote-control C-130."

"Or a crystal tumbler."

"What?"

"They can cause a lot of damage, is all."

"If you say so."

Was this knowledge from personal experience? Considering she'd thought about tossing a thing or two in his direction, she wouldn't be surprised. Taking a pair of towels from the cabinet, she piled them on a stool next to the tub along with a spare toothbrush.

"If you don't need anything else," she said, looking in his direction. Hammond had shed his dress shirt completely, and stood in his T-shirt studying the bloodied collar. Noelle struggled not to notice the way his biceps stretched his sleeves.

This sudden bout of awareness disturbed her. She'd never been one to check out other men. Of course, the fact that this was the first time a man had stood in her bathroom since Kevin probably heightened her sense of awareness. And while she didn't like Hammond, he was handsome. She had been struck by how much so when she'd checked on him during the night. He had been blessed with the most beautiful mouth she'd ever seen. Perfect Cupid's bow, full lower lip.

"What time do you have to be at Belinda's?"

His question jerked her back to the present. Dear God but she was having focus issues all of a sudden. "Not for a couple hours," she replied.

"Good. You'll have time to drive me to the airstrip."

Her stomach twisted a little. "So you're still planning to fly home today, then."

"What's the matter? Worried I changed my mind between the kitchen and here?" He grinned.

Something else she'd noticed this morning. His mouth was capable of an annoyingly attractive smile.

Noelle scoffed. "Hardly. I doubt you ever change your mind."

"Only if I'm well and truly persuaded."

The intimate atmosphere made the comment sound dirtier than it was. Noelle fought to keep a flush from blossoming on her skin.

"That's what I thought," she said. He'd stick to his decision, even if the idea was a bad one. Nothing she could say would change his mind.

Oh, well. He was a grown man. If he wanted to risk his safety, it was his concern. She started to leave. "Do you need anything else?"

"No. I won't be long." From the corner of her eye, she saw him start to shake his head, then close his eyes.

He probably doesn't think I can see him.

Once again, Noelle's conscience twisted her stomach.

"You know…" she started. "Belinda isn't going to be happy with you. She was expecting you for Thanksgiving dinner."

"I'm sure she'll survive." There was an odd note to his words. Disbelief or doubt?

I don't make a habit of staying where I'm not wanted. His comment seemed intent on repeating itself in her brain.

"Survive? Sure," she replied. "That doesn't mean she won't be disappointed. Thanksgiving is a big deal to her. God knows she cooks enough for the entire state—and we're talking about a woman who gave up cooking when Ned made his first million. She'll hunt you down if you aren't around to try her sweet potato casserole."

"There's an image," he said with a soft laugh.

"But not far off. I'm willing to bet she was up early making something special for you."

"Something special?"

"That's the way the Frybergs do things. Seems to me the least you can do is stick around long enough to try whatever it is."

Noelle watched as his eyelashes swept downward and he glanced at the tile floor. He had pretty eyelashes too. When he raised his gaze, his eyes had an odd glint to them. The light looked right through her, and her argument.

"Is this your way of asking me not to fly?"

"I'm not asking you anything," she immediately replied. "I'm thinking of Belinda's feelings."

What was supposed to be nonchalance came out sounding way too affected, and they both knew it. Truth was, she didn't want to deal with a guilty conscience should something happen. "Belinda likes you."

The corners of Hammond's mouth twitched like they wanted to smile. "Nice to know one member of the Fryberg family likes me."

"Don't get too flattered—Belinda likes everyone." Apparently, her conscience wasn't bothering her too much to stop being bratty.

To her surprise, he laughed. Not a chuckle, like previously, but a bark of a laugh that seemed to burst out of him unexpectedly. "Well played, Mrs. Fryberg. Tell me, are you always so upfront with your opinions?"

Honestly? Quite the opposite. She much preferred adaptation and assimilation to challenge. Hammond brought out an edge she hadn't known she had. "Not always," she replied.

"I'll take that as a compliment then." He crossed

his arms, causing the T-shirt to stretch tighter. "There aren't a lot of people in this world who would say boo to me, let alone challenge me as much as you have these past twenty-four hours. It's been very entertaining."

Noelle wasn't sure if she should be flattered or feel condescended to. "I wasn't trying to entertain you," she said.

"I know, which makes me appreciate it even more. You've got backbone."

So, flattered it was. "You're complimenting me for being rude to you."

"Not rude. Honest. I like knowing where I stand with people. You may not like me, but at least you don't pretend, which is more than I can say for a lot of people."

He may have meant to be complimentary, but his words struck her uncomfortably. They pressed on her shoulders along with his comment from earlier. If he was trying to prick her conscience this morning, it worked. She took a long look at him. Tall, handsome, arrogant, and yet... Maybe it was the concussion misleading her, or maybe the injury shifted a mask, but she was seeing something in his expression she hadn't noticed before. It almost looked like…

Vulnerability.

The chip slipped a little off her shoulder. "I don't dislike you," she said, toeing the tile. "Not entirely. Like, I'd feel bad if you crashed your plane and died or something."

"Your kindness overwhelms."

"What can I say? I'm a giver." They smiled at one another, the air between them thawing a little more. The guy wasn't so bad when he wasn't talking about gutting tradition.

"Seriously," she said, "I wouldn't want to see anyone—you—do anything foolish."

"So now you're calling me foolish, are you?"

"I—"

"Relax, I'm joking. I know what you were trying to say. And I thank you."

"For what?" She hadn't done anything special.

His expression softened like she had, however, and she saw the man she'd watched sleep. "Caring about my safety," he replied. "Not many peop— That is, I appreciate it."

A tickle danced across the back of her neck

at the gentleness in his voice. If he kept it up, they'd be friends before the bath water grew cold. "Does that mean you'll consider staying for dinner? I wasn't kidding about Belinda being disappointed."

"Well…" He ran his fingers across his mouth and along the back of his neck. "I'd hate to disappoint the woman who sold me her company. I suppose sticking around a few more hours wouldn't hurt."

"Good. Belinda will be glad."

"No one else?"

The cheeky question demanded a shrug in reply. "I might be a little bit relieved. Lack of blood on my hands and all. Enjoy your bath, Mr. Hammond."

She closed the door before he could see in her eyes that she was way more than a little relieved.

Or that she was starting to like him.

CHAPTER FOUR

JAMES ADDED A LOG to the fireplace. The wood smoked and sputtered for a moment, before being hidden by the flames rising from the logs beneath. Warmth wrapped around his legs. Legs that were now clad in khakis, thanks to Noelle. She'd cajoled the Nutcracker's concierge into opening the hotel boutique so he could buy a fresh change of clothing. The casual pants and plaid sports shirt were more stylish than he'd expected, a fact Noelle took great pleasure in mocking once he'd completed his purchase. His rescue elf had a terrifically sharp sense of humor.

Then again, so did he. Tossing retorts back and forth in the car had him feeling as much like his old self as the bath and clean clothes.

Behind him, cheers erupted in the downstairs family room. Someone must have made a good play. A politer man would head down and join the other guests, lest he be labeled unsociable. Since James had stopped caring what people thought of him when he hit puberty, he stayed upstairs. He was content sitting in one of a pair of wingback chairs, studying the fire.

"People were wondering where you were." Noelle's heels click-clacked on the hard wooden floor until she drew up beside him. "Don't tell me you're not a football fan. Isn't that against the law in New England?"

"Only a misdemeanor," he replied. "I'll be down shortly. I was enjoying the fire. It's soothing."

"Hmm. Soothing, huh?" Perching on the arm of a wingback chair, she looked up with a tilted glance. Before leaving the house, she'd swapped her sweatshirt for an angora sweater. The neon blue reflected in her eyes, giving them a gemlike glow. "Let me guess," she said, "you're not a fan of crowds either. Can't say I'm surprised."

"I don't dislike them," he replied. "But you're right, I prefer being by myself." It was easier that way. Less picking up on the negative vibes.

He shifted in his seat. The small space between the chairs caused their knees to knock. Laughing, they both pushed the seats back. "Let me guess," he said, "you love crowds."

"I don't love them, but they don't bother me either. I spent most of my childhood having to share my space, so I'm used to it."

An interesting choice of words. "You came from a big family then?"

"Not really."

Then with whom was she sharing space?

"Did you get enough to eat? There's more cornbread casserole if you'd like some."

"Dear God no," he replied. "Four servings is enough, thank you." Why such an abrupt change of subject? He was under the impression she was all about family. "I can't believe I ate as much as I did."

"That's what you get for sitting next to Belinda and her ever-moving serving spoon."

"Plus almost two days without eating." He literally had been the starving man at the buffet. The perfect match for Belinda's serving spoon.

Noelle wasn't joking when she said her mother-in-law cooked up a storm for the holiday. The woman must have served three times as much as the guests could eat. Granted, the turkey and side dishes were nothing like the five-star fare the family chef set out—on those rare occasions he and Jackson celebrated together—but James had enjoyed eating them ten times more. The food today came with wine and laughter and conversation. Real conversation. The kind where people debated, then joked the tension away. No stilted dialogues or pretend interest in each other's lives.

And not a single tumbler hurled across the room.

Funny how that memory had reappeared today, after twenty years of staying buried. Especially since it happened on Christmas Eve. Thanksgiving had been a Tiffany candlestick. Or had that been the dinner plate? The flying objects blended together after a while.

"You're frowning," Noelle said. "Is your head okay?"

"My head's fine." A faint headache at the base of his neck was all. The bulk of his dizziness had ebbed as well. Unless he whipped his head around quickly or hung upside down, he wouldn't have a problem.

"Guess that means you'll be able to fly home without a problem."

"Don't see why not," he replied. His original reason still stood. So long as he could control when and where he stayed, he would. "No sense overstaying my welcome, right?"

"Definitely not," Noelle replied. "Is it a long flight?"

"A few hours. One of the benefits of being the pilot, you save all that time waiting at the airport."

"No security pat down either. Is that why you fly? So you can avoid lines at the airport?" While she was talking, she slid backward off her perch and into the chair. The move left her sitting sideways with her calves balanced on the arm. "Wow, you really do hate people, don't you?"

Her smirk told him she was teasing. "Very funny," James replied. "I fly because it's more efficient. I don't like wasting time."

"Really? Who would have guessed?"

This time he smirked. Her sitting in such a cozy, casual position had made his muscles relax as well. He was at ease, he realized. An unusual experience outside the cockpit. The sky was the one place he felt truly at home. He would never tell that to anyone though. At thirty-nine-thousand feet, the sound of the engine roaring in your ears drowned out your thoughts. There was nothing to prove, nothing to forget.

"I was studying Belinda's mantel." He nodded toward the fireplace, and the collection of photographs and knickknacks that lined the thick pine. Diverting the attention away from himself once more. "Couldn't help noticing you and she have a lot of the same pictures."

"No big surprise, considering I married into her family."

Family was definitely the theme. The largest photograph was a portrait of a man in a military uniform smiling from the passenger seat of a truck. Pushing himself to his feet, James walked over to take a closer look. A copy of the photo was on Noelle's mantel as well. "Kevin?" he asked. He already knew the answer. Who else could it be?

"He emailed the photo from Afghanistan a few months before the accident."

His jeep flipped over. James remembered from

researching the sale. He'd been surprised to hear the Fryberg's heir had been in the military.

"He looks like he enjoyed being in the army."

"Guard," she corrected. "Signed up our senior year of high school." James heard a soft rustling noise, which he realized was Noelle shifting in her chair. A moment later, her heels tapped on the wood floor again. "He was so excited when his unit finally deployed. All he ever talked about was getting overseas. Ned and Belinda were crushed when they learned he'd been killed."

Was it his imagination or did all her answers go back to Ned and Belinda? "Must have been hard on you too."

"I was his wife. That goes without saying."

He supposed it did. It was odd is all, that she focused on her in-laws' grief instead of her own.

Then again, maybe it wasn't. Maybe that was how real families behaved.

The picture on the left of Kevin was from their wedding. The Fryberg quartet formally posed under a floral arbor. It too had a duplicate at Noelle's house. "How old were you when you got married anyway?" She looked about ten, the voluminous skirt of her wedding dress ready to swallow her.

"Twenty-one. Right after graduation. We were already living together, and since we knew Kevin was scheduled to leave after the first of the year..." She left the sentence hanging with a shrug.

No need to say more. "You didn't have a lot of time together."

"Actually, we had almost twelve years. We were middle school sweethearts," she added, in case that wasn't obvious. She smiled at the photograph. "I did a lot of growing up in this house."

"There you two are! Detroit's almost done letting everyone down." Belinda came strolling through the living room along with Todd Moreland, Fryberg's general manager. "I promised Todd here some pie for the road." When she saw he and Noelle were looking at her son's photo, she smiled. "I always liked how happy he looked in that photo."

"He was a real special kid," Todd added. "The whole company liked him. We always figured we'd be working for him one day. No offense, Mr. Hammond."

"None taken," James replied stiffly. "Everyone has their preferences." And it usually wasn't him.

"Noelle was filling me in on some of the family history," he said, turning to Belinda.

"You picked the right person for the job. She remembers more about the family history than I do at this point. In fact, she can tell you who those people in the portrait are. I forgot a long time ago."

"Ned's great-grandparents from Bamberg."

"See what I mean?" The older woman tugged at her companion's arm. "Come on, Todd. I'll get you that pie."

"So, keeper of the family history, huh?"

"Someone has to. Family's important."

"That, Mrs. Fryberg," he said, shuffling back to the chairs, "depends upon the family."

He shouldn't have said the words out loud; they invited a conversation he didn't want to have. Taking a seat, he steered the conversation back to her. "What about your family? Do you maintain your own history as diligently as your in-laws'?"

A shadow crossed her face. "Like you said," she replied. "Depends upon the family."

It appeared they had both dropped curious comments. In her case, she'd dropped two. Was it possible they had more in common than he'd thought?

Catching her gaze from across the space, he held it in his. Trying to tell her he understood. "What's that old saying about families? You can't live with them…you can't take them out and bury them in the woods."

"I don't think those are the words."

Her expression clouded again as she added, "Besides, you can't bury something you don't have." The words came out low and hesitant. Her gaze broke from his and returned to the photographs on the mantel as though she was speaking more to them than James.

Normally when a woman made coy remarks, he ignored them, seeing how coy was nothing more than an attempt at attention. Something about Noelle's remark, however, cut through him. There was weight to her words that spoke to a piece inside him.

Maybe that's why he decided to ask. "You don't have a family?"

Her sigh rattled signs in Chicago. "What the hell. Not like it's a secret.

"I was raised by the state," she said. "My mother left me in the town crèche on Christmas Eve and disappeared never to be heard of again."

That wasn't necessarily a bad thing, he thought. Better that she disappear altogether than sell you a fantasy and then unceremoniously pop the bubble.

He stared at the crease in his new pants. No wonder her comment affected him the way it had.

The two of them had more in common than she realized.

"Anyway, I grew up in the foster system. The Frybergs were the first real family I ever had. If it weren't for them, people would still be calling me the Manger Baby."

"The what? Never mind." He figured it out as soon as he asked. She said she'd been left in the crèche.

Something else dawned on him as well. "Is that how you got your name? Because you were found at Christmas?"

Her cheeks turned crimson as she nodded. "Nothing like advertising your past, huh? I shudder to think what they'd have called me if I were a boy."

"Trust me, I can imagine."

They both chuckled. When they were finished, he sat back in his chair and took a fresh look at the woman he'd spent the last twenty-four hours with. "It suits you," he said. "The name."

He wasn't surprised when she rolled her eyes. "So I've been told by half the town."

"Half the town would be right." There was a brightness about her that reminded him of a Christmas ornament. He could only imagine what she'd looked like as a kid. All eyes and luminosity.

No wonder Kevin Fryberg fell for her.

Knowing her story, a lot of things made sense now. Her loyalty. Her attachment to every tradition Ned Fryberg ever started.

He sat back in his chair. "You know, hearing all this, I've got to say I'm surprised Belinda sold to me when she had you around to take her place."

The muscle on her jaw twitched. He'd clipped a nerve. "I said the same thing. I suggested she retire, and let Todd run the place while he groomed me to be his replacement, but she said this was the best move for the store. Hammond's would give us the capital we needed to stay modern. Plus, she thought selling would give me more freedom to do other things. She didn't want me to feel trapped in Fryberg because I was tied to the business."

Interesting. Made sense. While Noelle professed loyalty now, she was also young, with a host of options in front of her. Better to sell the business while Belinda could control the deal. That's what he would do. His father as well. Hell, if James weren't so good at making money, Jackson probably would have sold the store years ago—and not because he wanted his son to have freedom.

Still, he could hear the disappointment in Noelle's answer. A part of her felt rejected. Cast aside. He knew that sting. It made him want to pull her into his arms for a hug, which was unsettling, since he didn't do comfort. And even if he did, she would deny the feelings.

Meaning they shared another trait in common as well: neither liked to show weakness.

"Look on the bright side," he said instead. "She could have fired you."

"You don't fire family."

"Speak for yourself, sweetheart. Not everyone is as family oriented as you are. There are as many people on the other side of the line who value profits over DNA."

She tilted her head. "I'm curious? Which side do you fall on?"

James didn't even have to pause and think. His answer was that reflexive. "The side that doesn't believe in family period."

Noelle stared at him. Unbelievable. No sooner did she catch a spark of warmth, then his inner Grinch came along to snuff out the flame.

"You do know how ironic that statement sounds, coming from the heir of Hammond's, right?"

Ask anyone in the industry and they'd tell you, Hammond's Toy Stores was the epitome of old-fashioned family values. Their history put Fryberg's hundred-year-old tradition to shame.

James's lashes cast shadows on his cheeks as he studied the palm of his hand. "Things aren't always what they seem," he said.

"They aren't? 'Cause I've studied Hammond's." And the last time she checked, Hammond's sure looked like a fifteen-decades-old success story. The Boston store dwelled in the same building where Benjamin Hammond originally opened it. Over the decades, the store had become a touchstone for people looking to recapture childhood innocence. Their window displays and decor was like walking into a magical piece of frozen history. And at Christmas time…

Noelle had seen the photos. It was the Christmas Castle, Santa's workshop and Rockefeller Center all rolled into one. "There's too much heart in your branding for it to have been pulled from a hat."

His reply was somewhere between a cough and a snort. "I'll let the marketing department know you appreciate their efforts. They put a great deal of effort into creating that 'heart.'"

She could feel the air quotations. There were exclamation points on the sarcasm.

"I hate to break it to you," he said, "but my family has made a small fortune selling a fantasy."

"For one hundred and fifty years? I don't think any company can fake their corporate culture for that long."

"Maybe once, a long time ago, someone believed in it," he said in a softer voice. "My grandfather or someone like that."

His fingers traced the plaid pattern on the chair arm. "Who knows? Maybe back then, life was different. But holidays are all manufactured now. There's no such thing as a 'family Christmas' except on TV. Divorce, dysfunction…most of the world's just trying to get through the day without killing each other."

Noelle didn't know what to say. She couldn't call him on his sarcasm, because he wasn't being sarcastic. He delivered his words in a flat, distant voice tinged with hopelessness. It took squeezing her fists by her sides to keep from hugging him. What was it he had said about glass tumblers?

"I'm sorry," she murmured.

"For what?"

Good question. She wasn't sure herself. "That you don't like Christmas."

Hammond shrugged before returning to his pattern tracing. "Don't have to like it to make money off it," he said.

"No," she said, "I don't suppose you do." And

Hammond did make money. Lots of money. So, he was right. Who cared if he liked Christmas or not?

Except that the notion left her incredibly sad. Noelle didn't know if it was the cynicism of his words or something else, but this entire conversation left a pang in her stomach. She couldn't look at Hammond without wanting to perch on his chair and press him close.

To chase away his sadness. Talk about silly. Twenty-four hours ago she disliked the man and now here she was thinking about hugging him? As though a hug from her would solve the problem anyway. She didn't even know if he was sad, for crying out loud. Imagine what he would think if she suddenly nestled up against that hard torso.

That she was crazy, no doubt.

Still, possible personal demons aside, she wondered how long it would take before Hammond's cynicism bit him in the behind? She didn't care how good a marketing team he had, a store that didn't believe in its own brand couldn't last. Sooner or later the phoniness, as he put it, would seep through.

You can only bury the truth of your feelings for so long before the truth wins out.

The corner of her gaze caught the photo on the edge of the mantel. Noelle turned her head.

And thought of Fryberg's. Without sincerity at the helm, the castle would truly become a cheesy tourist destination. Wouldn't take long after that for Hammond to close the store down, in favor of his giant shipping warehouse. The store was on borrowed time as it was. His cynicism short-ened the timetable.

"Bet if you spent time here, you wouldn't be so negative."

"Excuse me?"

Oh, jeez. She'd spoken out loud, hadn't she? The point had merit though. "The magic of the place has a way of growing on you," she said.

"Is that so?"

Interesting that he hadn't said *no.* "Yeah, it's so. Do you think this cottage industry of a town sprang up because people wanted to live in Bavaria again?"

Her question made Hammond chuckle. "The thought crossed my mind."

It crossed a lot of people's. "The people here love the holidays. You want to see the Christmas spirit you need to see tomorrow's Christmas season kickoff. It'll convert the most frozen of hearts into holiday fans."

A light flickered in his eyes, along with an emotion Noelle couldn't quite recognize, but made her pulse quicken nonetheless. "Are you asking me to stick around, Mrs. Fryberg?"

"No. I mean, yes. Sort of." Articulating herself would be easier if he weren't chuckling. "So you could see how we do Christmas, is all."

"I've seen how you do Christmas. Part of the celebration struck me in the head yesterday, remember?"

"I meant how the town did Christmas. I thought, if you spent time with people who enjoy celebrating Christmas, it might make you less cynical."

"I see. Worried my cynicism will kill the Christmas Castle sooner rather than later?"

In a word? "Yes," she replied. Wasn't he already turning things upside down in the name of efficiency?

Damn if he didn't chuckle again. A throaty rumble that slid under a person's skin and brushed across her nerve endings. The sound left goose bumps on Noelle's skin. "No offense to your Christmas magic," he said, "but I highly doubt a few gingerbread cookies and a tree lighting will make me less cynical."

He had a point. She probably was giving the magic too much credit. "Once a Grinch, always a Grinch. Is that what you're saying?"

"Precisely. I always thought he was misunderstood."

"As misunderstood as a man with a tiny heart could be," Noelle replied.

This time, instead of chuckling, Hammond let out a full-on laugh. "I wasn't trying to be funny," she said when he finished.

"I know. I was laughing at how easily you're abrupt with me. It's so damn refreshing."

So he'd said this morning. "I'm not trying to be," she told him. "The words keep popping out before I have a chance to mentally edit."

"Making it all the more refreshing, knowing it's organic." He settled back in his chair and assessed her with, based on the tingling running up her arm, what had to be the longest look in the world.

"You know, I have half a mind to bring you along when I fly out of here so you could follow me around and make snarky comments."

"Excu—"

"Don't worry, I'm kidding." He wiped the words away with a wave of his hand. "I have no desire to move you from Fryberg. *Yet*."

Noelle let out her breath.

"What's this about flying to Boston?" Todd asked. He and Belinda came around the corner from the kitchen. The general manager had on his coat and carried a plastic bag filled with Tupperware.

"You're not planning to fly back tonight are you, Jim? They showed Foxborough on TV and the rain looks miserable there."

Partially hidden behind the chair wings, Hammond winced at the nickname, leaving Noelle to fight back a smirk. If there was anyone who looked more unlike a Jim…

"I've flown in rain before," he said. "I doubt it'll be a problem."

"If you say so. All I can say is better you than me. That wind was blowing so strong the rain was sideways. Won't be much of a passing game, that's for sure."

"How strong is this wind?" Hammond asked, swiveling around to face the man. Noelle noticed he already had his phone in his hand. Checking the forecast, probably.

"No clue. They didn't say."

"Maybe you should stay like you planned," Belinda replied. "I would hate for you to be bounced around during a storm and hit your head again."

"I'm sure I'll be fine. We fly above the weather."

"What about you?" he asked Noelle, once the others had departed. "You want to ask me to stay again too?"

The sparkle in his eye caused a rash of awareness to break out along her skin. "I didn't ask you to stay. I *suggested* staying for tomorrow's Christmas Kickoff might change your mind about the holiday. There's a difference." One of semantics maybe, but she clung to the argument anyway. "Besides, you made it quite clear this morning that you make your own decisions. If you want to risk flying in the wind, that's your business."

She fought back a frown. That last sentence sounded a little passive-aggressive. It was his business and she didn't care—not that much anyway.

"You're right. It is my business," he replied.

Noelle watched as he tapped the keys on his phone and pulled up the Boston weather. An odd feeling had gripped her stomach. A cross between nervousness and disappointment. Something about Hammond had her emotions skittering all over the place. One minute she detested him, the next she felt a kinship. The man had turned her into a collection of extremes. It wasn't like her, being this mass of shifting energy.

Rather than continue staring, she turned to the pictures on the mantel. Kevin smiled at her from the Humvee and her insides settled a little. Good old Kevin who she'd loved for nearly fifteen years.

Loved like a brother.

No sooner did the thought rise than she stuffed it back down. How she felt about Kevin was her secret and hers alone. No one need ever know the truth.

Besides, she *had* loved him. He was her best friend. Her shoulder. Her rock. He'd given her so much. A home. A family. When she became his girl, her world went from being cold to one full of love and meaning. Kevin turned her into someone special. Wasn't his fault she couldn't feel the passion toward him that he deserved.

"Looks like you got your wish." Hammond's voice sounded above her ear. Startled, Noelle stepped back only to have her shoulders bump against his muscled chest, causing her to start again.

"What wish?" she managed to say as she turned around.

"Todd was right. There's a high-wind warning up and down the New England coast. Logan's backed up until the nor'easter moves on."

"What does that mean?" she asked. Focused on putting distance between their bodies, the significance of his words failed to register.

"It means…" He reached out and cupped a hand on the curve of her neck. His thumb brushed the underside of her jaw, forcing her to look him in the eye. The sparkle she saw in his left her with goose bumps.

"It means," he repeated, "that you're stuck with me another day."

It was the perfect time for a sarcastic remark. Unfortunately, Noelle was too distracted by the fluttering in her stomach to think of one. The idea of his continuing to stay around didn't upset her nearly as much as it had yesterday.

In fact, heaven help her, it didn't upset her at all.

James was disappointed when the barbed comment he'd been expecting didn't come. Instead, he found himself standing by the fire while Noelle went to tell Belinda he'd changed his plans. Again. Oh, well, what good was flying your own plane if you couldn't control your flight schedule, right?

He twirled his smartphone between his fingers. Christmas Kickoff, he thought with a snort. He'd go, but there was no way he'd change his thoughts on the holiday. The Hammond dysfunction was far too ingrained.

Turning his attention from the now empty doorway and back to his phone, James tried to settle the disquiet that was suddenly rolling in his stomach. He wished he could blame the sensation on being stuck in Christmas Land, but his phone screen told the truth. The conditions weren't that bad in Boston; he'd flown in worse dozens of times.

He'd used the wind as an excuse. To hang around.

He didn't rearrange his schedule on a whim for anyone, let alone a woman, and yet here he was making up reasons to spend additional time with Noelle Fryberg, a woman he was sure wasn't one hundred percent happy about the decision. He was breaking his own number one rule and staying where he might not be wanted. All because she made him feel energized and connected in a way no one ever had.

No wonder his stomach felt like it was on a bungee.

CHAPTER FIVE

Someone had shot off a Christmas bomb. How else could he explain it? Overnight, fall had disappeared and been replaced by poinsettias and tiny white lights. There were wreaths and red bows on doorways and evergreen garlands draped the fascia of every downtown building. It was even snowing, for crying out loud! Big, fluffy flakes straight out of central casting. An inch of the white stuff already coated the ground.

"What the heck?" he said as he looked out the passenger window of Noelle's SUV. "Did you drag a snow machine over from one of the ski resorts?"

"Nope. A happy coincidence is all," Noelle replied. "Makes a nice touch for the start of the Christmas season, doesn't it? Snow always puts people in the Christmas spirit."

"Keeps people off the roads too. People hate driving in snowstorms."

"Maybe back in Boston, but in this town, we deal perfectly fine with snowstorms."

"Residents maybe, but what about all those out-of-town shoppers?"

"Oh, I wouldn't worry about them," she replied.

They turned onto the main drag, where the bulk of the shops and restaurants were located. First thing James noticed was the steady flow of people looking into windows.

"See? The town will do very well economically over the next few weeks, weather or no weather."

"Yeah, but will they drive from downtown to the toy store?" That was the real issue. No one minded walking a few blocks; it was risking the roads that made people balk. Today, Black Friday, was the day retailers counted on to jumpstart their yearly profits. A healthy turnout was vital. "Conditions like this are one of the reasons why I want to push the online business," he said. "Bad weather encourages people to stay inside and shop online." Where there was a lot more competition for their attention.

Not surprisingly, she ignored his comment. "I wouldn't worry too much. We've got things under control."

She pointed ahead to where a bus stop had been decorated with a big gold sign that read Trolley to Christmas Castle Every Fifteen Minutes. "Like I said, we're used to snow. There's already a line too. Everyone loves to visit Santa's workshop."

The smugness in her voice begged to be challenged. "Crowds don't necessarily equal sales. Half the people coming to see the foolish window displays at the Boston store never buy a thing. Not a very good return considering how much we spend on them every year."

She gave him a long look. "If that's how you feel, then why continue having them? Why not scale back?"

"Because…"

James frowned. Why did he continue doing the windows on such a grand scale? Not even his own father wanted to continue the tradition. Yet, every year, he saw the numbers, and then turned around and approved something equally lavish for the following December. It was the one budget item where he deviated from his own rules of business and he didn't have a decent explanation.

"People have come to expect them," he replied. That was the reason. He was preserving Hammonds' reputation with the public. "Those window displays are part of the Hammond brand."

"I'm surprised you haven't figured out a way to support the brand in a less expensive way. Building brand new, custom animatronic exhibits every year is expensive."

Tell me about it, he thought. "Cutting back would send a negative message to the public. They might equate it with financial difficulties that don't exist." James could imagine how the business press might speculate.

"In other words, it's not always a good idea to mess with tradition."

"Unfortunately, no."

"You mean like Fryer and the Santa's reindeer corral at the castle."

Damn. She'd boxed him in. Quite neatly too.

Shifting in his chair, he tipped an imaginary hat. "Well played, Mrs. Fryberg. I see your point."

"I thought you might, Mr. Hammond," she said, nodding her head in return.

Neatly playing him, however, did not mean she was getting all her own way. "You still can't have people leaving Santa's workshop, and not reentering the store. The idea is to keep them around the toys as long and as much as possible."

He waited for a response, half expecting another argument. Instead, she daintily flicked the turn signal handle with her fingers. "Fair enough. What about Fryer?"

"Fryer?" Parts of the other day were still a bit fuzzy. James had to think a moment about whom she was talking about. Finally, he remembered. "You're talking about the giant stuffed moose eating up space at the rear of the store."

"Elk," she corrected.

"What?"

"Fryer. He's an elk, and people love taking selfies with him. In fact, customers have been known to bring friends specifically to see him. Much like your window displays."

So it was the moo—elk she wanted to save. Strange item to draw a line over. Then again, she did mention something about Ned Fryberg using the creature in his early ads and as he'd learned yesterday, his hostess had a very strong attachment to Fryberg history.

"Fine," he said. "The elk can stay. But only until I get a good look at the profit per square foot. If we need to redesign the floor plan, I make no promises."

"But he stays for now?"

"Yes," James replied, his sigh sounding more exasperated than he truly felt. "He can stay."

She turned and smiled. "Thank you."

That made twice in three days that she'd managed to convince him to bend on a decision. Granted, neither were major sticking points. Still, she had a better record than most of the experienced negotiators he'd faced.

Beginner's luck, he told himself. It definitely didn't have anything to do with how her eyes got bluer when she smiled.

He continued studying her after she'd turned her eyes back to the road. Today she was dressed for the holidays in a red sweater and a brightly colored scarf. Candy cane stripes, naturally. A matching knit cap sat on her head. The outfit made her look like a tiny character from *Where's Waldo*, only she'd stand out in any crowd, regardless of her size.

A blush worked its way into her cheeks as she sensed him studying her. "How's your head this morning?" she asked. "You never said."

"Better," he replied. Better than better actually. The spot around his stitches was still tender, but the dull ache had disappeared and he could bend and turn his head without the room spinning. "Being able to shower this morning helped." Nothing like being able to stick your head under a stream of water to erase the cobwebs. "Having a bed helped too. No offense to your sofa."

"I'm glad you were awake enough to climb the stairs this time," she replied. "I was thinking that considering how tired you were last night, it was a good thing you couldn't fly home after all."

"Yeah, a good thing." James forced his expression to stay blank. When they'd returned from Belinda's, he'd gone straight to the bedroom, telling Noelle he was too tired for conversation. In reality, he wanted the solitude so he could process his decision to stay. He wanted to say it boiled down to attraction. Noelle wasn't stereotypically beautiful—more cute really—but the more he studied her eyes, the more he found her gaze hypnotically compelling. If that was even a thing. And her curves…he did love those curves, no doubt about it.

Problem was, attraction didn't seem like a complete enough answer. It wasn't the challenge either, even though she clearly challenged him. He was drawn to her in a way that went beyond attraction. What that meant, he didn't have a clue, other than knowing he liked her in a way that was different from other women he'd known. Whatever the reason, he didn't like feeling this way. He didn't want someone getting under his skin. Didn't want the awkwardness when things inevitably blew up.

Why break his cardinal rule then by sticking around last night? To spend time with a widow devoted to her late husband and his family, no less?

Hell. Maybe he did want the awkwardness.

Maybe he had some subconscious desire to punish himself.

Certainly would explain a lot of things.

A flash of color caught his eye. They were passing an open-air market of some kind, the perimeter of which was marked off by a banner of rainbow-colored flags.

"That's the *Christkindlmarkt*," Noelle said. "It's German for Christmas market."

"Yes, I know. I've seen them in Europe."

"Really? Only other one I've seen is in Chicago. Ned and Belinda told me about the one they visited in Berlin. Sounded wonderful."

James watched as they passed a woman moving her collection of knit scarves out of the snow. "If you like flea markets," he said.

"It's a lot more than a flea market," Noelle replied. Even with his head turned to the window, he could feel her giving him the side-eye. It made his stitches tingle. "We hold the market every year. There are crafts, baked goods. Did you even spend time at the market in Europe? Or were you too busy studying the traffic patterns?"

"Contrary to what you might think, I don't analyze every retail establishment I visit. And no, I didn't have time to visit the market in Germany. My car drove past on the way to a meeting."

"No wonder you are being so derisive!" she said. "We'll visit this one on our way back from the store. Besides the castle, it's the linchpin of our Christmas Kickoff festival. One of the vendors, Heineman's Chocolatiers, has the most amazing hot chocolate you've ever tasted. Kevin and I made a point of visiting his stall first thing every festival. Mr. Heineman would never forgive me if I skipped it."

"God forbid you break tradition," James replied. The strangest flash of emotion passed through him when she mentioned Kevin. Not jealousy—he hadn't known Noelle long enough to feel possessive—but the sensation had the same sharp kind of pang. Like a tear in the center of his chest.

He'd been feeling a lot of odd things these past two days. Maybe that drone had jarred something loose when it struck him.

All he knew was the idea of Noelle and her beloved late husband strolling through the Christmas fair made his sternum ache.

* * *

"I owe you an apology. That was the most organized chaos I've ever seen."

Noelle's chest puffed with pride. Store management had spent years perfecting their Black Friday routine, so she knew James would be impressed. What she hadn't counted on was how his positive reaction would make her feel. She took his compliments as a personal victory. Unable to contain her smirk, she let the smile spread as she looked to the passenger seat. "I take it you no longer think of the castle as a fading tourist attraction then."

"I still think our retailing future lies online," he replied, "but I'll concede that you all know what you're doing here. Those handheld wish list scanners are genius."

"Thank you. Ned installed them shortly before he passed away."

Borrowed from the supermarket industry, the scanners let kids record items they fell in love with. The lists were downloaded to share with Santa as well as their parents. Moms and dads could purchase the items then and there and have them stored for pickup at a later date.

"We've boosted our Black Friday numbers by thirty percent since installing them," she told him. "Of course, our numbers drop a little at the back end, but we prefer to start the season high rather then sweat it out at the end of the quarter."

"Don't blame you there." He smiled again, and this time Noelle got a little flutter in her stomach.

Her assessment of his smile hadn't changed in the last twenty-four hours; if anything, she was finding it more magnetic. Especially when he let the sparkle reach his eyes. That didn't always happen. Noelle found those smiles—the ones with shadows—intriguing too.

Despite the voice warning her the shadowy smiles were the more dangerous of the two.

"When I was a kid, the store made paper lists. Kids wrote down ten items and put the letter in a mailbox for Santa. Parents could come by and pick up their child's list at the front desk."

James had taken out his phone and was typing a note. "This is much more efficient," he said.

"I'm sending a message to our logistics department about the scanners right now."

"I had a feeling the system would appeal to you. Although, I've got to admit…" She paused to back out of her parking space. "There was something special about folding up the letter and dropping it into that big red-and-white mailbox." Christmas always brought out the nostalgic in her. "Scanning bar codes doesn't feel the same."

"Even Santa's got to keep up with technology," James replied.

"Yes, he does. By the way, did you see how popular Fryer was with the crowd? I had a half dozen people ask me if we were bringing back our stuffed animal version."

"So you told me in the store. Twice," he replied, as he tucked the phone back into his coat. "I take it this is your way of saying 'I told you so.'"

"You've got to admit. I did tell you." A chuckle bubbled out of her, cutting off the last word. Didn't matter. He got the point.

In the grand scheme of things, Fryer's continued existence was a small victory, but one that made her happy. She'd saved part of Fryberg's, which was like saving part of her family.

"Don't hurt yourself gloating," James said.

His comment only made her chuckle a second time. Heaven help her, but she was starting to enjoy their verbal jousts. "I'm trying, but it's hard when I was so right. People really love that elk. We should have taken your picture."

"Why? For you to hang in your office?"

"Uh-huh. With a piece of paper underneath that reads The Time I Told James Hammond So." She waved her hand over the wheel as though painting the words in the air.

"Oh, well. Guess my memory will have to do."

From the corners of her eyes, she saw him shifting his position until he faced her. "Anyone ever tell you that you're cute when you're being smug?"

"No," Noelle replied.

The feel of his eyes on her turned her skin warm. It had been a long time since a man had studied her, let alone one with eyes as intense as his. She'd be lying if she didn't admit she found his scrutiny flattering. All morning long, she'd sensed him stealing glances here and there, checking her out as she reached for an item from a shelf or adjusted her rearview mirror. The sensation left goose bumps on her skin, not to mention a warm awareness deep inside her.

It felt good, being noticed by a man. That was, a man like him. Someone smart and savvy. Who took charge of a space simply by entering it. His scrutiny left her feeling decidedly female.

Plus, it kept her from feeling guilty about her own stolen glances. She'd been looking his way since their conversation in front of the fire.

She was stealing a look now.

"Getting ready to gloat more?" James's eyes had slid in her direction, catching her. Try as she might to stop them, her cheeks started to burn.

"No," she said. "I'm done gloating."

"Glad to hear it. Why the look then? You looked like you were about to say something."

Had she? "I was looking at your shirt," she replied. "You…" Her cheeks burned hotter. "You wear plaid well."

"Thank you." The compliment clearly took him by surprise, which was okay, because she was surprised she'd said it out loud. "I'm glad you like it since it's going to be a wardrobe staple while I'm here."

Interestingly, he didn't say anything about leaving. But then, the snow probably made flying impossible.

More interesting was how relieved she felt about his staying.

Again.

And heaven help her, it wasn't only the banter she was enjoying. She was enjoying James's company. A lot. "We can stop at the boutique and grab you a new shirt if you'd like."

"Are you saying you don't like this shirt?" he asked.

"Not at all. I mean, I like the shirt," she corrected when his brows lifted. "I told you, you look good in plaid."

"Thank you. You look good in…red-and-white stripes."

Sensing that another blush was working its way to the surface, she quickly turned her face to scan the left lane. "Color of the day," she murmured.

"Shouldn't it be black? Being Black Friday and all."

"Technically, maybe, but red is far more festive." They were stuck behind a returning trolley. Flicking her turn signal, she eased into the left lane to pass. A little boy with his face pressed to the window saw the car and waved. "I'm not sure a bunch of people running around in black would inspire Christmas spirit," she continued.

"Good point. All that really matters is that the red color stays on the people and not on my balance sheet."

"Said every retailer everywhere today."

"No one said we weren't predictable," he observed with a laugh.

"You can say that again," Noelle replied. Bad Black Friday jokes were as much a tradition as Santa in her office. Hardly surprising that a man raised in the retail industry knew his share of them. "Although not every retailer was born into a retail dynasty."

On his side of the car, James made what sounded like a snort. "Lucky me," he replied.

"I'm sure some people would think so. Ned

used to tell me about the early days, when his parents weren't sure the store would survive. He considered it a point of pride that Kevin would inherit a thriving business. I know we're not talking the same thing as a multimillion-dollar national chain..."

"Yeah," James said, reaching back to rub his neck, "if there's one thing my father knows how to do, it's make money."

"As do you. According to Belinda anyway. It's one of the reasons she chose to sell to Hammond's in the first place. Because she liked the idea that you would be stepping into your father's shoes. As she put it, the apple didn't fall far from the tree."

"That isn't necessarily a compliment," James replied.

No, thought Noelle. She supposed it wasn't. Especially if his father was like the man who'd arrived at their store two days ago. She thought him brusque and unsentimental. Absolutely hated the way he'd been focused solely on product and profit.

Oddly enough, James's comments today didn't upset her. Oh, sure, he was just as focused on profit and efficiency, but rather than annoy her, James's suggestions this time around had sounded incredibly astute. Probably because this time around, she liked him better.

Which might also explain why she detected a bitter edge to James's voice when she compared him to his father. "Don't you and your father get along?" she asked.

"Let's say my father does his thing, and I do mine," he said when she cast him a look. "It's a system that's worked quite well for us for a number of years."

Work or not, it sounded lacking. "I can't help but wonder," she said, "if some of these cynicisms of yours are exaggerated."

"I beg your pardon?"

"Well, you can't hate your family too much if you work for the family business."

He stiffened. "I work for the family business because I'm good at it. Like you said, the apple doesn't fall far from the tree. Not to mention that if I didn't, Hammond's wouldn't be a family business anymore," he added in a softer voice.

"There aren't any other family members?"

"None that are around," he said in a chilly voice. Clearly, it was a touchy subject.

Figuring it best to move on, Noelle focused on the rhythm of her windshield wipers going back and forth in the snow. Too bad the wipers couldn't swipe away the awkwardness that had overtaken the car.

As they got closer to downtown Fryberg, the road narrowed to one lane. Thanks to the snow, the already slower than normal traffic was reduced to a crawl. Only the castle trolley, which traveled in the bus lane, made any progress. Looking to the passenger seat, James was attempting to lean against the headrest without pressing on his stitches and not having much luck. His brow was furrowed and his mouth drawn into a tense line. Was he agitated because he was uncomfortable or from her uncomfortable question? Either way, it made Noelle anxious to see.

The sign for Bloomberg's Pharmacy caught her eye, giving her an idea. "Think your head can handle the snow?" she asked.

"It won't melt, if that's what you're asking," he replied.

"Good." With a flick of her directional handle, she eased the car to the right.

"From here until the central parking lot, traffic's going to be slower than molasses. I'll park at the drug store and we can walk."

James's frown deepened. "Walk where."

"To the Christmas market, remember?"

"Hot chocolate and gingerbread cookies. How could I forget?"

"You left out Christmas spirit," she said. "I thought maybe we could find you some. That way you don't have to rely on your marketing department to give your business heart."

"I told you yesterday, it's going to take a lot more than some midwestern Christmas craft fair."

Maybe, but a day at the market might make him smile. And for some reason, that was suddenly important to her.

Noelle swore the Christmas Kickoff got larger every year. At least the crowds did. Seemed to her that in middle school, she and Kevin darted from booth to booth without having to fight the flow of traffic.

James cut through the crowd like it was human butter. Hands in his coat pockets, he walked past the various stalls and vendors with such authority, the people naturally parted upon his approach. Noelle walked beside him and marveled.

Part of the deference had to be caused by his looks. He was, by far, the most handsome man there. The wind had burned his cheekbones pink while his hair and coat were dappled with snowy droplets. Dark and bright at the same time.

He looked over at her with eyes that refracted the light. "Where is this chocolate maker of yours?" he asked.

"I'm not quite sure." Rising on tiptoes, she tried to scan the aisle, but there were too many people taller than her. "In the past, Mr. Heineman liked to take a stall toward the rear."

"Then to the rear we go," he replied. "Like salmon heading upstream. This cocoa better be everything you claim it to be."

"Better. I promise, you'll be addicted." Mr. Heineman had a secret recipe that made the cocoa smooth and spicy at the same time.

"Addicted, huh? You're setting a pretty high bar, Mrs. Fryberg."

"It's not high if it's true," she told him with a grin.

And there it was. The start of a smile. Like a lot of his smiles, it didn't reach his eyes, but they had all afternoon. After the way he'd closed off in the car, she was determined to pull a bona fide grin out of him before they were finished.

She'd contemplate why the mission mattered so much later.

"Coming through!" Four teenage boys wearing matching school jackets were pushing their way through the crowd with the obnoxious aggression of teenage boys. The tallest of the four crashed his shoulder into Noelle. As she pitched sideways, an arm grabbed her waist. Instead of taking a face full of snow, she found herself pressed against cashmere-covered warmth.

"Looks like it's your turn to get knocked over," James said, his chest vibrating against her cheek as he spoke. "You all right?"

"Right as rain." His coat smelled faintly of expensive aftershave while his shirt smelled of her orange body wash. A subtle combination that tempted a woman to rest her head. Okay, tempted *her*. Instead, she pressed a palm to his shoulder to steady herself. "We do have a habit of falling around each other," she said. "Thank you for catching me. In this crowd, I might have gotten trampled."

"That would definitely kill your Christmas spirit." Among other things. "Maybe you should hold on in case you get jostled again."

Noelle stared at the arm he was holding out for a moment, then wrapped a hand around his biceps. The curve of his muscles was evident even through the coat, reminding her that his vulnerability over the past few days was an exception. All of a sudden she felt decidedly dainty and very female. Her insides quivered. To steady herself, she gripped his arm tighter.

"Hey? Everything all right?"

He was looking down at her with concern, his eyes again bending the light like a pair of brown-and-green prisms.

"F-f-fine," she replied, blinking the vision away.

"You sure? You seemed a little unsteady for a moment."

"Must be your imagination. I'm steady as can be," she told him. Or would be, so long as she didn't meet his gaze.

She met his gaze.

"Are you sure? Because we could…"

It had to be a trick of the light because his pupils looked very large all of a sudden.

"Could what?" she managed to ask.

"Go…" His gaze dropped to her lips.

Noelle's mouth ran dry.

CHAPTER SIX

"GO," JAMES REPEATED. "I mean… Back to the sidewalk. Where it's not as crowded." He shook the cotton from his brain. Was that what he meant? He'd lost his train of thought when she looked up at him, distracted by the sheen left by the snow on her dampened skin. Satiny smooth, it put tempting ideas in his head.

Like kissing her.

"Don't be silly," she replied. For a second, James thought she'd read his mind and meant the kiss, especially after she pulled her arm free from his. "It's a few inches of snow, not the frozen tundra. I think I can handle walking, crowd or no crowd. Now, I don't know about you, but I want my hot cocoa."

She marched toward the end of the aisle, the pom-pom on her hat bobbing in time with her steps. James stood and watched until the crowd threatened to swallow her up before following.

What the hell was wrong with him? Since when did he think about kissing the people he did business with? Worse, Noelle was an employee. Granted, a very attractive, enticing one, but there were a lot of beautiful women working in the Boston office and never once had he contemplated pulling one of them against him and kissing her senseless.

Then again, none of them ever challenged him either. Nor did they walk like the majorette in a fairy band.

It had to be the drone. He'd read that concussions could cause personality changes. Lord knows, he'd been acting out of character for days now, starting with agreeing to stay for Thanksgiving.

It certainly explained why he was standing in the middle of this oversize flea market when he could—should—be working. Honestly, did the people in this town ever do anything at a normal scale? Everywhere he looked, someone was pushing Christmas. Holiday sweaters. Gingerbread cookies. One vendor was literally making hand-blown Christmas ornaments on the spot. Further proof he wasn't himself, James almost paused because there was one particularly incandescent blue ornament that was a similar shade to Noelle's eyes.

The lady herself had stopped at a booth selling scented lotions and soaps wrapped in green-and-gold cellophane. "Smell this," she said, when he caught up with her. She held an open bottle of skin cream under his nose, and he caught the sweet smell of vanilla.

"It's supposed to smell like a Christmas cookie," she said. "What do you think?"

"I like the way your skin smells better." He spoke automatically. It wasn't until her eyes looked down and away that he realized how his answer sounded.

"I'm not a huge fan of vanilla," he quickly amended. "I prefer citrus smells."

"We have a holly berry scent which is fruity," the vendor said, reaching for a different sample. "Maybe you'll like this one better."

"I don't think..." Before Noelle could finish,

the saleswoman grabbed her hand and squirted a circle of pale pink cream on her exposed wrist. "Scents smell different on than they do in the bottle," she said as she massaged the lotion into Noelle's skin. "That's why it's always best to try the sample out before you buy. What do you think? Fruity, eh?"

She started to lift Noelle's wrist, but James intercepted. Keeping his eyes on hers, he raised her wrist to his nose and inhaled. Traces of berry mingled with the orange blossom. "Better," he said.

Noelle was staring at him, her lower lip caught between her teeth, and he instantly thought about nibbling her lip himself. "But you don't need it," he finished. The scent and/or the nibbling.

He, on the other hand, was definitely going to see a neurologist when he got back to Boston.

For the second time, she slipped free of his touch. "I—I'll have to think about it," she told the saleswoman.

"Don't think too long," the woman replied. "I sell out every year."

"We'll keep that in mind," James replied. Noelle had already moved along.

"Sorry about that," he said when he caught up. He noticed she'd stuffed both her hands deep into her coat pockets. "I didn't realize she was going to make me smell your skin."

"The lady was definitely working for the sale."

"Vendors at these things always are."

They were conveniently ignoring that James was not a man who people made do anything, as well as the fact he could have sampled the scent without brushing the tip of his nose across her skin. "I hope my comment didn't stop you buying something."

"Of course not. I know what I like and don't like."

"I'm sure you do," he replied. In this case, as she'd twice demonstrated, she didn't like sharing any more personal space with him than necessary.

Message received. Copying her, he stuffed his hands in his pockets.

"Heineman's Chocolatiers is straight ahead," she said, nodding toward the red-and-white-striped stall fifty yards away. "Doesn't look like there's too much of a line either."

Considering the crowds, that didn't bode too well for the chocolate. One would think the greatest cocoa in the world would have lines a mile long.

A burly man with gray bushy hair peeping out from beneath a Santa hat waved to them as they approached. "There's my Noelle! I wondered when I would see you!" Leaning over the table, he wrapped Noelle in a hug. His arms were so massive she nearly disappeared from view. "It's good to see you, child. Merry Christmas!"

Noelle replied something that sounded like "Murry Chrfmaf!" before breaking free. "It's good to see you too. I've been dreaming about your hot chocolate since last December."

"You say that every year."

"I mean it every year. You know it's not Christmas until I have my Heineman's Hot Chocolate fix."

James got a twinge in his stomach. Noelle wore a smile brighter than anything he'd seen on her face. Brighter than anyone had ever smiled around him actually.

"This is James Hammond," she said. "His company purchased the store."

"I read in the paper that Belinda had retired and sold the business. I'm surprised she lasted as long as she did after Ned's death. The store was always more his, and with Kevin gone..."

The man paused to wipe at a spot of dried chocolate with his hand. An impromptu moment of silence.

"I'm surprised she didn't have you take over," he said once the moment ended.

"I'm afraid I haven't worked long enough to have the experience," Noelle said. "I also didn't have the kind of money Mr. Hammond put up."

"I read that in the paper too. Nice to meet you, Mr. Hammond."

"Same here," James replied. "Noelle has been raving about your hot chocolate all day. She swears it has magical properties."

"I didn't say that," Noelle shot back. "I said it tasted magical."

"Auch! You and that man of yours were always saying that. Ever since you were in junior high.

"Did she tell you about her man?" he asked James.

"Some," he replied.

The old man nodded. "Kevin Fryberg. Belinda's son. Fine young man. A true hero."

"So I've been told."

"Left a hole in the town when he died," Mr. Heineman continued. "A huge hole. Can't imagine how Belinda coped. Or this one."

Noelle was looking down and fingering a tiny tear in the plastic tablecloth. Her cheeks had turned a darker shade of pink. "Mr. Heineman…"

But the vendor didn't get her hint. "Did she tell you how he died?" James shook his head, eager to learn details his research couldn't. "Truck rolled over and blew up while he was trying to pull one of his men free."

A true hero, like the man said. Bet he was a great guy through and through. The kind of guy who was easy to fall for. "Pretty amazing," James replied.

"The whole town loved him," Mr. Heineman repeated. "Isn't that so?"

Noelle, who still hadn't said anything beyond his name, nodded. "Everyone," she repeated softly.

"And this one… Joined at the hip, the two of them. Kevin Fryberg and the little Manger Baby. They made the perfect couple."

"Mr. Heineman…" This time, the words came out a little stronger, whether because of unwanted memories or the Manger Baby comment, James wasn't sure. Probably unwanted memories, considering how she started twitching the moment Kevin's name came up.

Personally, James wanted to hate the man—Kevin—but he couldn't. It was impossible to hate a saint. Instead he jammed his hands down deeper into his pockets.

"I don't mean to be rude, but I promised Mr. Hammond hot chocolate, not a trip down memory lane." Noelle did her best to smile brightly as she cut the older man off. "I need to prove to him that the drink's worth bragging about."

"Of course it's worth bragging about. Two cups of Heineman's Hot Chocolate coming right up."

"Prepare to be blown away," she said to James with an enthusiasm she no longer felt.

"My taste buds can hardly wait."

"Go ahead and joke. I will be vindicated."

Naturally, his responding smile didn't reach his eyes.

Dragging James to the market had been a bad idea. If she hadn't let his eyes get to her in the first place, they wouldn't have had to stand here listening to Mr. Heineman go on and on about Kevin. Normally, the man's effusiveness didn't bother her; people always talked about Kevin. Their marriage. His heroism. Being Kevin Fryberg's widow was part of who she was. This afternoon though, Mr. Heineman's reminiscing was too much like a spotlight. It left her feeling guilty and exposed.

Oh, who was she kidding? She was feeling guilty and exposed before they ever reached Mr. Heineman's booth.

It was all James's fault. Him and his stupid, sad, kaleidoscope eyes. Twice now, he'd looked at her in that intense way of his, and twice she'd had to move away before her knees buckled. Twice, she'd held her breath thinking he might kiss her. Which was stupid, because if a man like James wanted to kiss a woman, he would simply go ahead and kiss her.

And, since he hadn't kissed her, he obviously didn't want to. A point she should feel relieved over, but she didn't. She felt foolish. Mr. Heineman waxing on about her great love affair only made her feel worse.

James's voice pulled her from her thoughts. "Seems you and your late husband made quite an impression," he said.

"After a dozen years of buying hot chocolate, I should hope so." Her attempt at lightness failed, so she tried again. "That's the kind of person Kevin was. Everyone loved him. He didn't even have to try."

"Some people are naturally lovable," he replied.

"Only some?" Something about his comment struck her as odd. Looking over at him, she waited for his answer only to get a shrug.

"Not everyone is on that side of the bell curve," he said.

"Bell curve? What the heck's that supposed to mean?"

Mr. Heineman's arrival prevented him from answering. "Here you go. Two cups of Fryberg's finest hot chocolate. On the house," he added, when James reached for his wallet. "To celebrate you buying Belinda's company."

"That's very kind of you."

The old man waved off the compliment. "My pleasure. Besides, it's the least I can do for my longest and most vocal customer. You come back later in the season, okay?" he said to Noelle.

"Don't I always, Mr. Heineman?" There were customers waiting behind them. Leaning over the counter, she gave the chocolatier another hug and left him to his business.

"Moment of truth," she said to James. "What do you think?"

He took a long sip.

"Well…?" She was waiting to drink herself until she heard his verdict.

James smiled. "This is good. Like truly good."

"Told you." Her thrill at seeing his pleasure was ridiculously out of proportion. "And here you thought I was exaggerating."

"Yes, I did," he replied, taking another, longer sip, "and I take every thought back. This chocolate definitely qualifies as amazing. What's in it?"

"Beats me. Mr. Heineman won't share the recipe with anyone. Claims he'll take the secret to his grave." She took a sip and let the familiar delicious thrill wash over her. "That'll be a dark day for sure."

James was studying the contents. "I can't believe no one's suggested he bottle and sell it. A drink this good, sold in stores, would make him a fortune."

"He's been approached. So far as I know he's turned all the offers down. I think he feels it would lose what makes it special if you could have the drink all the time."

"Sort of like a store celebrating Christmas every day?" James replied.

"That's differ— Jerk."

He chuckled, forcing her to nudge him with her shoulder. It was like poking a boulder, and had as much effect, which made him chuckle again. Noelle hated to admit it, but the sound slid down her spine with a thrill similar to the cocoa. It was certainly as smooth and rich.

Quickly she raised her cup to her lips, before her reaction could show on her face. "You know exactly what I mean," she said.

"Yes," he replied, "I do. He's also a rare bird. Most people would willingly sell out for the sake of a fortune."

"Would you?" she asked.

His face had *Are you joking?* written all over it. "Weren't you listening yesterday? Hammond's already has."

Right. Their family fortune made by selling a fantasy.

Cocoa mission accomplished, the two of them began walking toward the market entrance. As their arms swung past one another, Noelle's muscles again tensed with a desire to make contact. She thought back to the lotion display and the way James's nose brushed her skin. Barely a wisp of contact, it nonetheless managed to send tingles up her arm. Now here she was having the same reaction from the memory.

Didn't it figure? All day, she'd been pulling away from his touch only to wish for it now, when the moments had passed.

But what if she touched him?

She snuck a glance through her lashes. Walking in the snow had left James's hair damp and shiny. At the back of his head, where the doctor had woven the stitches, there was a tuft sticking out at an odd angle. What would he do if she reached over and smoothed the unruliness with her fingers? Would his pupils darken the way they had before?

Would his eyes fall to her mouth?

She took a long swallow of cocoa. Thoughts like those were only asking for problems. Better to purge them from her brain.

"Before Mr. Heineman brought us our cocoa, you were talking about bell curves," she said. "You never explained what you meant."

He shrugged. "Ever take statistics?"

"In high school."

"Then you remember how results look when

plotted for a spectrum, with the bulk of responses falling in the middle."

"The bell." Memories of mountain-shaped graphs popped into her head. "With the outliers on either end. I remember."

"Same thing works with personality traits, intelligence, etc. Most people are average and therefore fall in the middle. Every now and then, however, you meet someone who skews way over to one side. Like your late husband. He was clearly an outlier when it came to being well liked."

Noelle thought of how Kevin could charge a room with his presence. "He had a lot of personality. Like a big, enthusiastic teddy bear. It was easy to get caught up in his energy." So much so, a person could misread her own emotions. "All the Frybergs are like that."

"Having met Belinda, I know what you mean."

"I wonder where I would have fallen on the bell curve if I hadn't been with Kevin," she mused. "Probably in the middle." The poor little orphan girl dropped in the manger.

"Are you kidding?" They were passing a trash

can, so he took their empty cups and tossed them away. "You are definitely an outlier."

"Don't be so sure. I'm talking about me without the Fryberg influence."

"So am I," he replied. "From where I'm standing, you'd be impressive, Frybergs or not."

Noelle was surprised the snow didn't melt from the blush spreading across her body. He'd looked her square in the eye as he spoke, with a seriousness to his gaze that matched his voice. The combination made her insides flutter. "Really? I mean, th-thank you." She cringed at the eagerness in her voice. Sounded like she was leaping at the approval.

Still, she'd been entwined with the Frybergs for so long. It was the first time anyone had ever suggested she was unique on her own. Well, Belinda had, but that was more maternal affection.

"You're welcome," he replied. "And..." He reached over and smoothed her scarf. Right before pulling away, his gloved fingers caught her chin. "Really."

Her insides fluttered again. Double the speed this time.

"Wait a second."

They'd resumed their walk when the rest of his comment came back to her. "Didn't you say you were on the other side of the bell curve? That doesn't make sense."

"Why not?" Again, he shrugged. "We can't all be warm, huggable teddy bears. The world needs cool and efficient as well."

"True," Noelle replied. Why did his indifference sound forced, though? He was leaving something out of his comparison. Whatever that something was, its unspoken presence made her want to tell him he was wrong.

She settled for saying nothing. For his part, James seemed happy to see the subject dropped. "Traffic's eased up," he noted.

He was right. With the snow done and the bulk of the day over, there were fewer cars on the road. Most of the tourists were either on their way home or warming up before the evening festivities. "They'll start blocking streets for the Santa Light Parade soon." A few hardy souls were already setting up lawn chairs. "Santa will drive his sleigh down Main Street to light the town tree, and then Christmas season will be officially here."

"And you all do this every year?"

"Like clockwork," she told him. "I'm not the only one who takes traditions seriously. You've got to admit it definitely kicks up the Christmas spirit."

"I'll admit the town has a certain marketable charm to it, but I still prefer Boston and its other three hundred and sixty-four days."

"Marketable charm? You spend a day surrounded by Christmas and that's the best you can come up with?" Worse, he still had those far away shadows in his eyes. "You really don't like Christmas, do you? I know..." She held up a hand. "We covered this last night."

They were coming up on the Nutcracker Inn. The hotel had been decorated to look like a real gingerbread house. "So much for my theory that Fryberg's enthusiasm could inspire anyone."

"Sorry." To her surprise, his apology sounded truly sincere. "You shouldn't take it personally. When it comes to Christmas..."

He paused to run a hand over his face. "Let's

say my history with the holiday is complicated, and leave it at that."

In other words, sad. After all, people didn't hate the holidays because of happy memories.

"And here I thought I was the one with the juicy Christmas story," she said. "In fact, we're passing my birthplace now."

She pointed to the old nativity scene which had been relocated to the Nutcracker's front lawn. "Back when I was born, Mary and Joseph hung out in the park next to the Christmas tree. The Nutcracker took them in a few years ago."

"I'll refrain from pointing out the irony," James said.

"Thank you." Pointing to the baby in the center, she said, "That's where they found me. Bundled up next to the baby Jesus. I guess my mother thought he'd keep me warm."

They stopped in front of the display. "Anyway, a group of people walking by noticed there were two babies, alerted the authorities and a Fryberg legend was born."

"Manger Baby," James said.

"Exactly. And you say your Christmas history is complicated."

Noelle could make light of it now, but when she was a kid? Forget it. Being the odd man out, even at home. The foster families were decent enough and all, but she was never truly a part of them. Just the kid the state paid them to take care of. Whose mother abandoned her in a plaster nativity display.

Thing was, she could justify her mother giving her up, but why couldn't she have picked a fire station or somebody's doorstep? Why did she have to go with the cliché of all clichés on Christmas Eve, thus saddling her child with a nickname that wouldn't die?

"I hated that nickname," she said. "Every Christmas, without fail, someone would dredge up that story, and that's all I'd hear on the playground."

"I'm sorry."

"Don't be." Reaching across the gap separating them, she touched his arm. "I've gotten over it. People don't call me the name anymore, haven't since I was in high school." Or maybe they did, and she didn't notice because she'd had the Frybergs.

James looked down at her hand on his arm. Feeling her fingers begin to tingle with nerves, Noelle moved to break away only for him to cover her hand with his. "It's a wonder you don't hate Christmas as much as I do," he said. "Considering."

"Never even crossed my mind." She stared at the manger. "Christmas was never a bad holiday. I mean, yeah I got stuck with that nickname, but there was also all of this too."

With her free hand, she gestured at the decorations around them. "How can you dislike a holiday that makes an entire town decorated for your birthday?

"Besides," she added. "There was always Santa Claus. Every year, the school would take a field trip to Fryberg's and we'd tell him what we wanted. And every year, those very toys would show up under the tree.

"I found out when I was in high school that Ned Fryberg made a point of granting the low-income kids' wishes," she said. "But when I was six or seven, it felt like magic."

"At six or seven, everything seems like magic," James replied. Noelle could feel his thumb rubbing across the back of her hand. Unconsciously, probably, but the caress still comforted. "But then you grow up and stop believing."

"In Santa Claus maybe. Doesn't mean you have to stop believing in holiday magic. I believe that special things can happen at Christmas time. Like Ned making sure kids got their gifts. People come together during the holidays."

She waited for James to chuckle, and give her one of his cynical retorts. When none came, she looked up and saw him staring at the manger with sad, faraway eyes. "They also rip apart," he said in a low voice.

CHAPTER SEVEN

JAMES'S WORDS—or rather the way he said them—caught her in the midsection. Taking her free hand, she placed it on top of his, so that he was caught in her grasp. "Ripped apart how?" she asked.

"My parents broke up on Christmas," he replied. "Christmas Eve actually. I woke up on Christmas morning and my mother and my little brother were gone. Moved out."

"Just like that? Without a word?"

"Not to me."

Wow. Noelle couldn't imagine. At least she'd been a newborn when her mother dropped her off. Unable to notice the loss. "How old were you?"

"Twelve. Justin, my brother, was ten."

Definitely old enough to understand. She tried to picture James coming downstairs that Christmas morning and discovering his world had changed. "I'm sorry," she said, squeezing his hand. The words were inadequate, but she couldn't think of anything else.

"It wasn't a complete surprise. Whenever my parents got together it was a drunken screamfest. Mom liked her whiskey. Especially during the holidays," he said with a half smile. "And Justin had always been her favorite, so..." He shrugged. Noelle was beginning to realize it was his way of shaking it off whenever the moment got heavy. Or in this case, touched too close to a nerve.

"I'm sure she would have..." She stopped, realizing how foolish what she was going to say sounded. Mothers didn't always want their children; she of all people should know that. "Her loss," she said instead.

The right side of James's mouth curved upward. "From the woman who's only known me for seventy-two hours. And disliked me for at least twenty-four of them," he added, his smile stretching to both sides.

"Meaning I've warmed up to you for forty-eight. Besides," she added, giving a shrug of her own, "I don't have to know you for a long time to realize your mother missed out on knowing you.

Same as my mother. Far as I'm concerned, they both didn't recognize what they had."

He squeezed her hand. Even trapped between her hands, his grip was sure and firm. Noelle felt it all the way up her arm and down to her toes. "Are you always this positive?" he asked.

"Me? Positive?" She laughed. "Only by necessity."

She let her gaze travel to the nativity set again. "For a long time, I dreamed about my mom coming back. She didn't have to take me away with her…"

"Just tell you why she left you behind."

Noelle nodded. He understood. "But she didn't. So, what else can I do but focus on being happy without her? Best revenge and all that, right?"

"You're right," James said. A chill struck her as he pulled his hand free from hers. Before the shiver could take true hold, however, gloved fingers were gripping her chin, and gently lifting her face skyward. James's eyes had a sheen to them as he smiled down at her. "Your mom lost out. Big time."

It might have been the nicest thing a man—anyone really—had ever said to her. While the Fry-bergs—and Kevin, of course—complimented her, they always made a point of avoiding any mention of her mother. For as long as she'd known them, her past had been the great elephant in the room. Known but not spoken aloud.

She'd had no idea how good having her past acknowledged could feel. "Yours did too," she said, meaning it. "Your brother might be a modern-day saint for all I know, but your mom still missed out. On the plus side, though, at least your father didn't."

He dropped his hand away. "That, I'm afraid is debatable."

While he sounded self-deprecating, she'd clearly said the wrong thing. There was a cloud over his features that hadn't been there before. It made Noelle's stomach hurt. "I'm…"

"It's all right," James said, holding up a hand. "My father isn't the most lovable man himself.

"It's all right," he repeated. Noelle waited for the inevitable shrug to punctuate the sentence; she wasn't disappointed.

James was wrong though. It wasn't all right. The

implication that he wasn't lovable wasn't right. Granted, she'd only known him a few days, but the man she was standing with right now seemed very lovable indeed.

She couldn't help herself. Rising on tiptoes, she wrapped her arms around his neck and pulled him into a hug. He stiffened, but only for a moment before sliding his arms around her waist.

"I think they're both idiots," Noelle whispered in his ear before laying her head on his shoulder. One of James's hands slid up her back to tangle in her hair.

They fit together well, thought Noelle.

Scarily so.

"What was I supposed to do? I mean, the guy's mother left him behind. On Christmas Eve, no less. I had to offer some kind of solace, didn't I?"

The photograph on the nightstand smiled knowingly. Kevin always did know when she was over-justifying. He would listen patiently, and when she finished talking, cock his head and say, "Who you trying to convince, Noelle? Me or you?"

"Me," she told the memory and flung herself

face-first across the bed. Why else would she be in her bedroom talking to a picture?

Letting out a long breath, she splayed her fingers across her plaid duvet. The fresh air and snow had taken their toll. Fatigue spread through her body, causing her to sink deeper into the down filling. If she lay here long enough, she'd fall asleep.

James wouldn't care. He was locked in his own room, having retreated there as soon as they returned home. His head was bothering him, he claimed.

Could be true. Embarrassed was more like it though. Who wouldn't be when one of their new employees suddenly starts clinging to them in the middle of Main Street?

He'd hugged her back though. With warm, strong arms that made her feel safe all over. "Like the ones you used to give," she told Kevin.

Except for the way she'd flooded with awareness.

There had been a moment, when James slid his arm around her shoulder, that she swore the awareness was mutual. Apparently not. If James had wanted her, she thought, tracing the threading on her comforter, he would have kissed her. He wouldn't have retreated to his bedroom alone.

"Sorry," she said to Kevin. "S'not like I'm looking to move on or anything. It's just I haven't been kissed in a long time—by a man, your mom doesn't count—and the idea is kind of nice."

Especially if the kiss came from a man with a mouth as beautiful as James's.

"You had a pretty mouth too, Kev," she said. Everyone in town used to say his smile was brighter than a Christmas tree. Once, when they were in high school, he'd taken her skiing, and face-planted in the snow getting off the ski lift. His laughter could be heard all over the mountain. God, but she missed that laugh.

She missed him. The private jokes. The Friday Old-Time Movie Nights.

"None of this would be a problem if you were here." She certainly wouldn't be drawn to her boss-slash-houseguest.

But, as her eyelids started to close, it was damp cashmere teasing her cheek, not brushed flannel, and the memory of warm arms cradling her close.

Kevin's voice sounded in her ear. *Who you trying to convince, Noelle? Me or you?*

By all rights, James should have gone straight to bed, risen early and called a taxi to take him to the airport before Noelle was up for breakfast. Steps one and two went according to plan. Step three, on the other hand, had run into some difficulty. Instead of doing his preflight check, he was sitting on Noelle's leather sofa downing coffee number two and staring at her mantel.

She'd hugged him.

Flirting, kissing, sexual aggression, those he could handle. If Noelle had thrown herself at him, he would have gladly reciprocated, and the two of them would be waking up in tangled sheets.

But a hug? Hugs were tender. Caring. They reached into vulnerable parts of you and offered compassion. How was he supposed to respond?

He'd hugged her back, that's how. Hugged her and took the comfort she was offering.

And when she put her head on his shoulder, it was like all the air had suddenly rushed to his throat. He'd nearly choked on the fullness. The last time anyone had bothered to comfort him was…

He couldn't remember. Certainly long before his mother left. God knows, she'd checked out on him long before that. His father even earlier. Was it any wonder he couldn't take the moment further?

Or were you afraid she'd say no?

The thought made his shoulders stiffen. Rejection had never been an issue before. Then again, a woman had never hugged him before either, or left him feeling so…so exposed. That made him want her even more, and he didn't mean sexually. He wanted to make her smile. Her eyes light up like a Christmas tree. To give her a dose of that magic she believed in so strongly.

Dear God. His mouth froze against his mug. He sounded like a sappy teenager. Could it be he was falling for Noelle?

"It can't be," he said.

"Can't be what?"

Noelle stood on the stairway in her Wisconsin sweatshirt and a pair of flannel sleep pants.

Baggy plaid pants that obliterated her curves. He hated them.

"James? Everything okay?"

He blinked. "I was looking at your pajamas. They're very…" He sought for a decent adjective. "Plaid."

"Thank you," she replied, padding down the last couple steps. Barefoot, James noted. "I wasn't expecting you to be awake this early," she continued. "And you're dressed."

"You sound surprised. I didn't think you'd want me wandering around your kitchen in my briefs."

"Now that would have been a surprise. Is everything okay?"

"Huh?" James missed the question. He was too busy studying her bare feet. They were runner's feet—no painted toes for her—and to his horror he found them as attractive as the rest of her.

"I asked if you were feeling all right," she repeated.

"I'm fine. Why wouldn't I be?"

"Well, you didn't look good last night when you booked it to bed. I was worried you overdid it and made your headache return."

Dammit. Did she have to ask with concern increasing the vibrant blue of her eyes? It made his chest squeeze again, like yesterday.

"I'm fine," he said. "No headache. I got up to check the forecast."

"Oh." Was that disappointment darkening her eyes? "And what did you find out?"

"Actually..." He'd been too busy arguing with himself to look at his phone. It lay dormant on the coffee table.

"Is there coffee left?" Noelle asked.

He nodded, embarrassingly relieved that he didn't have to look quite yet. "I made a whole pot."

"Great. I'm going to grab a cup. Give me yours and I'll get you a refill." She held out her hand and waited while he finished the last swallow. "You can tell me about the weather when I get back."

Okay, the pajama bottoms weren't so bad after all, James decided as he watched her walk to the kitchen. Although, he would much prefer her bare legged.

The woman was definitely under his skin, big time.

Leaning forward, he picked up the phone and

pressed the weather app. As the radar loaded on his screen, he saw it was clear all the way to the coast. No excuse against flying home.

Fantastic, he thought, shoulders feeling heavy.

What a difference a few days made. Two days ago he couldn't wait to get out of the place. Now here he was dragging his feet.

Again.

"So, what's the verdict?" Noelle asked as she came around the corner.

Handing him one of the mugs, she took a seat in the opposite corner and waited.

"Smooth sailing," he replied. "Not a snowflake in sight. I'm back to thinking you had a hidden snow machine yesterday for ambience."

"Wouldn't surprise me if Ned considered it," she replied. "I know at one point he was looking for a way to make snow in July."

"Did he?"

"Apparently years ago he used soap flakes, but they got in the water and caused all sorts of problems. After that, Belinda put the kibosh on summer snow plans."

"Good thinking." He was beginning to think

Ned Fryberg had been more than a little on the eccentric side. Envy twisted in his stomach. "Must have been fun, hanging out at their house as a kid."

"More like insane," she replied with a grin. "Ned was forever coming up with ideas. And they weren't all for the store. He went crazy at home too. You should have seen the to-do he made over Halloween. One year, he turned their living room into a haunted tableau. Kevin and his mom played haunted mannequins." James tried to picture the scene in his head. "What were you?" he asked.

"A flying monkey. Ned thought scary mannequins should be bigger than the fifth graders."

"I'm afraid he had a point there." Turning sideways, James rested his elbow on the back of the sofa, and propped his head with his hand. "I bet you made an adorable flying monkey."

"Scary! I was supposed to be scary!"

"Were you?" He waited while she sipped her coffee, noting her cheeks had grown the tiniest bit pink.

"No," she replied. Leaning in, she set the mug on the coffee table. The action brought along the orange blossom scent James had come to associate only with her. He breathed in deep through his nostrils. "I'm not surprised," he said once she'd left his senses. "I can't picture you as anything but adorable."

"Explains why we decided to decorate only outside the following year," she said, the blush James had been trying to deepen coming through. "Anyway, Ned was always coming up with something different. The neighborhood kids loved coming to the house to get candy."

"They sound like a fun family," he said. A true Rockwell painting. "My parents had the housekeeper pass out the candy." Bags of Hammond's brand goodies assembled by employees and doled out from a silver tray.

A hand suddenly covered his. Noelle's eyes were incandescent with unreadable emotion. "I'm sorry—I didn't mean to send us down that road again," she said.

"Road?"

"You know, our collective lousy childhoods."

James knew. But he wanted to hear how she framed the conversation.

"Bad enough we opened up all those wounds last night." She paused, reached for her coffee then changed her mind and pulled back. "I hope I didn't make you feel uncomfortable when I hugged you."

A loaded question. Depended upon her definition of uncomfortable.

"No," he lied. "Not at all."

"Good." He could hear her relief. "Because the moment seemed to call for one, you know? I didn't mean to overreach."

"You didn't," he told her. *You were the first person I'd ever shared my childhood with.*

Her eyes widened, and for a brief second, James wondered if he'd spoken his thoughts aloud. "So, you didn't go to bed early because you were avoiding me?"

Yes, I did. "Don't be silly. I had work to do, and I was tired."

"That's a relief. I… That is, we were…" A frown marred her features as she stared at their joined hands. "I wanted yesterday to jumpstart your Christmas spirit, not make things all awkward between us."

"They didn't make anything awkward," he told her. "As for the hug...it was nice. I liked it."

Soon as the words were out, his insides relaxed with a vengeance, as if they'd been gripped by tension for weeks, not a few days. He played with the fingers holding his. "I enjoyed spending time with you," he added.

"Me too," she said softly. "Even if we did get off on the wrong foot."

"More like wrong feet," James said, smiling. He took a good long look at her.

With one leg tucked under her body, she looked small and delicate against the dark leather. Only she wasn't delicate, was she? She was as resilient a person as he'd ever known. Strong, smart, loyal, gorgeous. A rare package.

Suddenly it struck him. Why he couldn't leave.

"What are you doing tonight?" he asked her.

As he suspected, her eyes got wide again. "Nothing. Why?"

"Because," he said, "I'd like to take you to dinner." And he knew the perfect place too.

"Dinner? You mean, like on a date?" From the

look on her face, the question caught her by surprise. A good surprise, he hoped.

"Exactly like a date. Two minutes ago, we both said we enjoyed each other's company. I don't know about you…" Lifting his hand, he risked brushing the hair from her face. "But I'd like to continue enjoying it a little longer."

Wow. Noelle didn't know what to say. She'd gone to bed last night convinced she'd embarrassed both of them by hugging him, that this morning he would be flying back to Boston as soon as possible. Instead, he was asking her out.

"But you're my boss," she blurted out. "Isn't that against some kind of rule?"

James chuckled. Noelle hated when he chuckled because the rumbling sound tripped through her every time. "I promise, where we're going, we won't run into a single coworker."

"Is that so?" Goodness, when did her voice grow husky? She sounded breathless.

"Absolutely. What do you say? Spend a few more hours with me? We can call it a thank-you for taking me in during my time of need."

His fingers were brushing her cheek again. Feathery light touches that made her mouth dry and turned her insides warm and liquid. Who exactly was supposed to be thanking whom in this proposal?

"All right," she said, fighting to keep from closing her eyes and purring. His touch felt that good. "I'd love to have dinner with you."

"Fantastic. You have my word you won't regret a single second. This is going to make your Christmas Kickoff look like a roadside yard sale."

She laughed. Good to know his audacity was alive and well. "I'll have you know I happen to like yard sales."

"You'll like this better. Now…" To her dismay, he took both his touch and the hand beneath hers away. "Why don't you go get dressed while I make the arrangements? If we hurry, we'll have time to walk around before the show."

Show? There weren't any shows going on in Fryberg. The closest performances she knew of were at least a two hours' drive away.

"Are we going to Chicago?" she asked.

James was on his feet and taking her coffee cup.

A man in command. "Not Chicago. I'm taking you to Radio City Music Hall."

"Radio what?" She'd heard wrong. "Isn't that in New York City?"

"Yes, it is," he replied. "Which is why you'd better hurry and get dressed."

CHAPTER EIGHT

SIX HOURS LATER found Noelle sitting in the back of an airport town car on her way to Manhattan, and wondering when—or if—her head would stop spinning. New York City for dinner? That was the sort of thing they did in movies. Yet there was the Empire State Building on the skyline ahead. And the Statue of Liberty alone on her island.

James's hand brushed her knee. "You haven't said much since we left the airfield. Everything okay?"

"I can't believe I'm actually in New York City for dinner" was all she could manage to say. "It's..."

"Amazing?"

"Yes. And overwhelming. When you said dinner, I never dreamed you meant—is that the Freedom Tower?" She pointed to a gigantic building with a large antenna, on top of which waved an

American flag. She'd seen pictures of the structure built to replace the Twin Towers, but they were nothing compared to the real thing. "It's huge. Even from this far away."

"That was the idea," he replied before shifting a little closer. "To make a statement to the rest of the world about our resilience."

"They won't keep New York down."

"Precisely. New York Strong, as we'd say in Boston," he replied. He shifted again and unbuttoned the top of his coat. Noelle caught a glimpse of pearl gray. Before leaving Fryberg, they'd stopped at the boutique so he could purchase another set of clothes, the plaid, he'd said, having worn out its welcome. The soft color was a toned-down version of the executive she'd met three days ago. That man, she thought with a smile, would never have flown her to New York.

His hand slid along hers, breaking her train of thought. "Would you like to see it up close?" he asked.

"Careful how often you ask the question. I want to see everything up close."

Now that she'd accepted the ginormousness of

where they were, excitement was quickly replacing disbelief. "I've always dreamed of going to New York ever since I was a little girl, but never got the chance."

"Never?"

"I almost went. Once. Right after Kevin and I got engaged. There was a merchandising conference I thought of attending."

"What happened?"

"The conference conflicted with an awards banquet Kevin had to attend. People expected me to be there too, so I cancelled. I could always go to Manhattan another time. Wasn't like the city was going to go anywhere."

"At least not last time I looked," James replied. "And now you're here."

"Now I'm here." She sat back against the leather seat and watched the traffic. Despite being the middle of the afternoon on a Saturday, the streets were lined bumper to bumper, with more cars than ten Fryberg Christmas Kickoffs. Everywhere she looked, buildings reached toward the sky. Big, square buildings jammed with people. She could feel the city's energy pulsing through the limousine's windows. It was fantastical.

Next to her, James was watching the window as well, his long fingers tapping on the armrest. He looked quite at home with the traffic passing by them. Same way he'd looked at home in the cockpit of his plane. Noelle had watched him the entire flight, his deftness at the controls far more interesting than the ground below. Surely he knew how gracefully he moved. If he didn't, the universe really should hold up a mirror for him to see.

"What?" He turned his face to hers. "Why are you staring at me?"

"Thank you," she replied, the words bubbling out of her. "For today."

"You haven't seen anything worth thanking me for yet."

Was he kidding? They were passing the biggest Christmas billboard she'd ever seen that very minute. "I don't have to see anything," she told him. "Being here is already amazing."

His eyes really did turn into sparkling hazel diamonds when he smiled. "You ain't seen nothing yet. You, Noelle Fryberg, are going to get the full New York Christmas experience."

"I can't wait."

It wasn't until she felt his squeeze that she realized they were still holding hands. Their fingers were entwined like puzzle pieces. Yet again they fit together with unnerving perfection.

James instructed the driver to pull over at the corner of Fifth and West Thirty-Third. Looking at the block of office buildings, Noelle frowned. "I might be a New York City virgin, but even I know this isn't Radio City Music Hall."

"There's no moss growing on you, is there?" James replied. Opening the door, he stepped outside and offered her a hand. "Since we have time before the show, I figured you'd enjoy a bird's-eye view of the city. Watch your step."

A blast of cold east coast air struck Noelle as she stepped onto the sidewalk. If not for James's warm hand holding hers, she might have shivered. His grip, however, left her impervious to the wind. "Bird's-eye view?" she said. "I don't under... *Ohhhh!*" Spying the crowd ahead, it clicked where they were. The Empire State Building.

"Precisely. Best view in the city, if you don't mind getting cold."

What a silly comment. "I'm from the Midwest, remember?" she replied. "We invented cold. Or have you already forgotten what it was like walking around yesterday?"

Despite James's warnings of cold, the outside observation deck was lined with tourists. The two of them had to wait before finding a space near the rail. When they finally made their way to a viewing spot, Noelle leaned as close to the barricade as possible. Below, the city spread for miles. She squinted past the rooftops and spotted Lady Liberty. From up there, the majestic statue looked no bigger than an action figure. "It's like standing at the top of the world," she said, only to cringe a little afterward. "Not that I'm being clichéd or anything."

"Hey, phrases become cliché for a reason." A pair of arms came around to grip the rail on either side of her, blocking the wind and securing her in a cashmere cocoon.

Noelle's fingers tightened their grip. She could feel the buttons on his coat pressing through hers, letting her know how close he was. So close that she need only relax her spine to find herself propped against his body. Did she dare? If she did, would he wrap his arms tighter? Her stomach quivered at the thought.

"I wonder if you can see the Christmas tree from the other side," she said.

"The one at Rockefeller Center? I haven't a clue."

Turned out she didn't need to slouch, because James stepped in closer. "Want to know a secret?" he whispered in her ear. His breath was extra warm against her cold skin. "I've been to Manhattan dozens of times over the years and this is my first visit to the top of the Empire State Building."

"Really?" The sheepish nod she caught over her shoulder made her smile. "You're a virgin too?"

Several heads turned in their direction, earning her a playful shoulder nudge. "Say it a little louder," James replied. "There are a couple of people below that didn't hear you."

"Okay. James Hammond is a—"

The rest of her sentence died in a giggle as he grabbed her by the waist and pulled her to him. Her head leaned back against his collarbone. "I'm glad we could experience this together," she told him.

For a second there was silence, then his voice was back at her ear. "Me too," he murmured. Noelle swore he brushed the shell of her ear with his lips.

Like a kiss.

They took their time on the deck, making sure they saw all four views. Each was spectacular in its own right, and Noelle decided that if her tour ended then and there, it would still be an unforgettable day. "You really need to stop thanking me," James said as they left the observation deck. "I'm feeling self-conscious."

"Then you shouldn't have sprung for such a marvelous day," she told him. "Isn't the whole point of a day like today to make a woman feel grateful?"

She meant it as a tease, but he took her seriously, looking down at her with eyes filled with sincerity. "Not this time," he said. "Not you."

If they weren't trapped in a line of tourists, Noelle would have kissed him then and there.

The crowd herded itself downstairs and into the gift shop. "I see they've got the traffic flow issue managed," she remarked, hoping shop talk would distract the fluttering in her stomach. It didn't help that James's hair was windblown. The bonded strands around his stitches stuck out at an angle. "Considering all their years of practice, I'd be disappointed if they didn't," he replied.

Noelle only half listened. She was too distracted by those errant strands. Her fingers itched to run through them. Because those mussed-up strands looked all wrong, she argued. If she were him, she'd want someone to adjust his appearance, right?

"Hold on a second." Grabbing his arm, she stopped him from heading toward the doorway. "Let me…" As gently as possible, she combed his hair smooth, making sure her fingers barely grazed the bump on the back of his head. "Much better."

Did she just purr? Wouldn't surprise her. Stroking his hair was nearly as soothing as being petted herself.

"You realize the wind is going to mess up my hair again the second we step outside."

"Then I'll simply have to fix it again." She smoothed a patch around his ear, which was really an excuse to continue touching him.

Her reward was a smile, and a brush of his fingers against her temple. "Well, if that isn't incentive to spend the day stepping in and out of the wind, I don't know what is. Now, what do you say? Should we continue exploring?"

Noelle shivered. Explore could mean so many things. Whatever the meaning, she had the same answer. "Absolutely," she said. "Lead the way."

They were walking out of Radio City Music Hall when James's phone buzzed. "Maybe you should answer," Noelle said. "That's what? The fourth call today?"

While she was flattered he considered her to be the higher priority, she knew from experience that not all calls could be ignored. "Generally speaking, people only bother the boss on weekends if there's an emergency."

"And what makes you so sure these calls are from the office?" he asked. "How do you know I don't have an expansive social life?"

Like a girlfriend back in Boston? The thought passed as quickly as it popped into her head. James wasn't the type to play around. He was, however, the type to work all hours. "Okay, Mr. Social Life," she challenged, "what would you be doing right now if you hadn't been stuck with me all weekend?"

"A person can be dedicated to his job and have a social life, I'll have you know. And I'm not stuck with you."

Still, her point had been made and he pulled out his phone. "I was right. Nothing that can't wait," he said. He rejected the call. Not, however, before Noelle caught the name on the call screen—Jackson Hammond—and the frown that accompanied it.

Curiosity got the best of her. "You don't want to talk to your father?"

"Not particularly," he replied. "I'm sure all he's

looking for is a trip update. I can fill him in when I get home."

Ignoring the unexpected pang that accompanied the words *get home*, Noelle instead focused on the rest of his comment. "I'm sure he wants to hear how you're feeling as much as he cares about the trip."

The sideways glance he sent her said otherwise. She thought about what he said yesterday, about his father and he doing their own thing. "He does know about your accident, doesn't he?" she asked.

James shrugged. "Word's gotten to him by now, I'm sure. I left a message with his 'protégé' that I was detained by a drone attack. She makes sure he's kept abreast of things."

"So you haven't spoken to him at all since your accident?"

"No." He stepped aside to let her exit the building first. "I told you," he continued, once he joined her, "my father and I aren't close. We don't do the family thing. In fact, I think I've made it pretty clear that the Hammonds are the anti-Frybergs."

Selling the world a clichéd myth. So he'd told

her. Ad nauseum. "Still, your father is trying to reach you. You don't know it's all about business."

"I know my father, Noelle. When I was a kid and broke my leg, he didn't come home for two days because he was in Los Angeles meeting with a distributor."

Poor James. "How old were you?" Not that it mattered. A child would feel second-best at any age.

"Twelve and a half."

Right after his mother left. A time when he needed to feel wanted and special. Her heart clenched on preteen James's behalf. Being abandoned by her parents sucked. Still, James had something she didn't, and she needed to point that out. "He came eventually. I know it doesn't sound like much," she said when he snorted, "but I would have killed for even that much parental attention."

"Don't take this the wrong way, but you got the better end of the deal. At least you knew where you stood from the start."

"More like where I didn't stand. My parents were out of my life from day one. So long as your father is around, you still have hope for a relationship."

Up until then, the two of them had been strolling the sidewalk. Now James stopped to look at her and for a moment, Noelle saw the twelve-year-old boy who'd been struggling to keep his hurt at bay. "Why hope for something that won't happen?"

And yet he did hope. She saw how his eyes flashed when she'd suggested his father might be worried.

"Never say never," she replied. "You can call me naive, but there's always hope. Look at me. For years, I burnt my Christmas wish on wanting a family, and then the Frybergs came into my life and poof! My wish came true."

"What do you wish for now?"

"I—" She resumed walking. "We're talking about you, remember?"

"We're also talking about hopes and dreams. You said you used to wish for a family. Since your wish was granted, you must hope for something else. What is it?"

"Peace on earth."

"I'm serious," he said.

"So am I." Every year, she, like every Fryberg's employee, filled out her Christmas wish list, and asked for large, conceptual things like peace or good health for all. There was no need for her to hope for anything personal. After all, hadn't she'd gotten everything she wanted when she'd become Noelle Fryberg? What more could she want?

James took her hand.

"This conversation is getting way too serious," he said. "Today is supposed to be about you getting the New York Christmas Experience. What did you think of the show?"

Noelle shook off her somberness with a laugh. "I loved it." She loved how he described the day with capital letters more. "If I were six inches taller, I'd start practicing my high kicks so I could audition."

"That's something I'd pay to see—you kicking your leg past your ears. I had no idea you were that limber," he added, leaning in to her ear.

Noelle's knees nearly buckled. It wasn't fair, the way he could lower his voice to the exact timbre to zap her insides. "Who said anything about ears? Waist-high is more like it.

"S'all a moot point anyway," she added. "With my size, I'd be more likely to get cast as one of the elves."

"And a right adorable one at that."

Noelle tried to shove him with her shoulder. Unfortunately, the impact had no effect. Instead, she found herself trapped against his side when he snaked his hand around her waist. The position left her arm no choice but to respond in kind and slip her arm around his waist as well.

"I mean it," he said, adding a side hug for good measure. "First thing I thought when I saw you was that you were Belinda's attack elf. So much feistiness in such a tiny package."

"I'm not sure if I should be flattered or actually try to attack you," she replied. With her luck, she'd end up wrapped in both his arms.

"Definitely flattered," he told her. "My second thought was I didn't know elves could be so beautiful. Are your knees all right?"

They wouldn't be if he kept purring compliments in her ear. "Careful," she purred back. "Keep up the sweet talk, and I'll get a big head."

"You deserve one. I've never met a woman like you, Noelle."

"You must not get out much."

Once more, he stopped, this time to wrap a second arm around her. Noelle found herself in his embrace. Heavy-lidded heat warmed her face as his eyes travelled to her mouth. "I'm not joking," he said. "You're an original."

If this were Fryberg, his features would have been hidden by the early darkness, but being the city that never slept, she could see his dilating pupils beneath his lashes. Their blackness sucked the breath from her lungs. She parted her lips, but couldn't take more than a shallow breath. Her racing heart blocked the air from going farther.

"I want to kiss you," she heard him say. "Right here, on this sidewalk. I don't care if people stare or make rude comments. I need to kiss you. I've wanted to since I—"

"Shut up, James." She didn't need to hear any more.

Standing on tiptoes, she met him halfway.

* * *

Kissing was something James thought he had a handle on. He'd kissed dozens of women in his lifetime, so why would kissing Noelle be any different?

Only it was different. With other women, his kisses had stemmed from attraction. He'd kissed them to stoke his sexual desire—and theirs. But he'd never *needed* to kiss a woman. Never had a bone-deep ache to feel their mouths on his.

The second his lips met Noelle's, a feeling he'd never felt before ballooned in his chest. Need times ten. It was the blasted hug all over again. Talking about his father and hope, she'd ripped open a hole inside him and now he couldn't get enough, couldn't get *close* enough.

Which was why he surprised himself by breaking the kiss first. Resting his head against her forehead, he cradled her face in his hands as they came down to earth.

"Wow," Noelle whispered.

Wow indeed. *Wow* didn't come close. "I think…" He inhaled deeply, to catch his breath. "I think we should get some dinner."

Noelle looked up her lashes. Her brilliant blue eyes were blown black with desire. "Is that what you want?" she asked. "Dinner?"

No.

And yes.

Some things were meant to simmer. "We've got all night," he said, fanning her cheek with his thumbs. The way her lips parted, he almost changed his mind, but inner strength prevailed. "Dinner first," he said with a smile. "Then dessert."

She nodded. Slowly. "All right. Dinner first."

"Wow. That might be one of the first times this weekend that you haven't disagreed with one of my suggestions." Maybe miracles could happen.

"What can I say?" she replied. "I'm hungry. Although..." The smile on her face turned cheeky as she backed out of his embrace. "Since you decided to postpone dessert, I'm going to make you work for it."

Her words went straight below his belt. Snagging a finger in the gap between her coat buttons, he tugged her back into his orbit. He leaned in, feeling incredibly wolfish as he growled in her ear. "Challenge accepted."

As seemed to be the theme of the past few days, James was completely wrong about the restaurant. He made their reservation based on an internet article about New York's top holiday-themed restaurants and wrote off the writer's ebullience over the decor as a marketing spin. For once, though, spin matched reality.

"Oh. My." Noelle gave a small gasp as they stepped inside. The place was completely done in white and gold to resemble an enchanted winter forest. Birch branches trimmed with tiny white lights formed a wall around the central dining room, making it look as though the tables were set up on the forest floor. There were Christmas ornaments and stockings strung about, as well as fluffy cottony-white snow on the window edges.

"Talk about a winter wonderland," Noelle said.

Indeed. Silly as it was, he actually felt the need to hold her hand tighter, in case some woodland creature tried to whisk her away. This was what she'd call magical. "I'm glad you like it," he said.

"Like it? It's unreal." She had her phone out and was snapping away at the various objects. Suddenly, she paused. "I'm not embarrassing you, am I?"

"Not at all." She was enchanting. "Take as many photos as you want. We'll be eating in a different room."

She frowned, and James almost felt bad for disappointing her. *Almost.* "You mean we're not eating in the forest?"

"Mr. Hammond requested a table in our crystal terrace," the maître d' informed her. He gestured to the elevator on the other side of the birch barricade. "Upstairs."

"We're eating on the roof," Noelle said a few moments later. He smiled at her disbelief as she stated the obvious.

Actually a glass atrium, the famed Crystal Terrace was decorated similarly to downstairs, only instead of recessed lighting, patrons ate under the night sky.

"I figured since this was our only meal in the Big Apple you should eat it with a view of the skyline," he told her. "By the way, this time you can see the Rockefeller Christmas tree. *And* the Empire State Building."

"Amazing."

Letting go of his hand, she moved toward the window while he and the maître d' exchanged amused glances.

"I had a feeling you'd like the view," James replied. He waited until the maître d' had disappeared behind the elevator doors before joining her at the glass. Noelle stood like a child pressed to a window display with her hands clutching the brass guardrail. Her lower lip was caught between her teeth in wonder. James stood behind her and captured her between his arms, the same way he had on the observation deck. "As good as the Fryberg town tree?" he asked.

"The Empire State Building really is red and green. I've read about how they projected the colors, but I had no idea they would be so vivid. The building looks like a giant cement Christmas tree."

"I'm not quite sure that's the analogy the city was going for, but…"

"I love it. Thank you for bringing me here."

Still trapped in his arms, she whirled around to face him. Up close, her smile knocked the wind out of him. He had to swallow before he could find his voice.

"I thought we agreed this afternoon that you could stop thanking me."

"We did, but a place like this deserves a special thank-you." She slipped her arms around his neck. "Makes sense now, why you wanted to have dinner. I'd have been disappointed if I'd learned... Are we the only people here?"

He was wondering when she'd notice. "No. There's a waiter and a bartender on the other side of the room."

"I don't mean the staff. I mean dinner guests. The other tables are empty."

"Are they, now?" He pretended to look over his shoulder. The Terrace only housed seven tables; the limited seating was part of how the place got its exclusive reputation. All seven tables were unoccupied.

"Well, what do you know. So they are empty," he said before turning back to her. "Must be because I booked them."

"You what?" Noelle's expression was worth every cent he'd paid too. Her eyes widened, and her lips formed an O. She looked so charming; he had no choice but to press a kiss to her nose.

"You know how I like efficiency," he told her. "Service is so much better when you don't have to compete with other patrons for the server's attention. Besides, I wanted to give you something special since you took me in these last few days."

"I was under the impression flying me to New York was the something special," she replied. "This is…"

Shaking her head, she slipped from his arms. "Do you do this sort of thing often? Buy out restaurants?"

James wasn't sure of the right answer. Had he gone too far? The impulse had popped into his head when he'd read the internet article. Yes, it was over the top—this whole day was over the top—but he'd wanted to make it memorable.

Face it: he'd wanted to impress her. Because he liked her. And how else was he supposed to compete with a dead war hero who gave her the family she'd always dreamed of?

"I didn't mean to make you uncomfortable," he replied. "If you want, I can tell the maître d' to open the other tables…"

"No." She shook her head again. "You went to a lot of trouble, and I'm sounding ungrateful. It's just that you didn't have to do all this. Any of this. I would have been perfectly happy having dinner with you at the Nutcracker."

"I know. I told you, I wanted to do something special. To make you feel special. Because I kind of think you're worth it. Hell, after kissing you, I know you're worth it."

He scuffed the ground with his foot. Stumbling for words wasn't like him. But once again, she had him feeling and thinking uncharacteristically.

"Thank you," Noelle replied. Unlike the other times, she spoke in a gentle, tender voice that hung in the air. "No one has ever put so much effort into trying to impress me. Ever. You've made me feel very special. I think you're crazy. But you make me feel special."

James smiled. So what if he was crazy? The satisfaction he was feeling right now far surpassed that of any deal or successful investment. "So does this mean you'll stick around for dinner?"

"What do you think?" she replied.

Turning to the first table within reach, James pulled out a chair. "After you."

CHAPTER NINE

"HERE'S WHAT I THINK." It was an hour later, and the wine had loosened Noelle's tongue. "I think that you're not as anti-holiday as you claim."

"I'm not?"

"Nope." Giving an extra pop to the *p*, she leaned forward across the table. Shadows cast by the flame in the hurricane lamp danced on the planes of James's cheek, giving his handsome features a dark and mysterious vibe. She'd been thinking about this for a while, analyzing the clues he'd dropped. Tonight's rooftop surprise sealed her theory. "I think you're sentimental and I think you're a romantic," she told him.

He rolled his eyes. "Why? Because I bought out a restaurant? Hate to break it to you, honeybunch, but that doesn't mean I'm romantic—it means I'm rich and trying to seduce you."

And he was succeeding. Not even the wine and

duck with truffles could wash the kiss they'd shared off her lips. James kissed like a man in charge. She might have met him halfway, but there was no doubt who dominated whom once the kiss began, and frankly, so caught up was she in the moment, that she didn't care. She liked being overwhelmed.

Right now, however, she didn't like him distracting her.

"Why are you so quick to paint yourself negatively?" she asked, getting back on track. "Last time I checked, a person could be rich and seductive and a sentimental romantic. This restaurant is only one example. The entire day..."

"Again rich and..."

"Trying to seduce me. I know," she replied.

James reached for the bottled water to pour himself a glass. "So far, I've got to say that your argument isn't too compelling."

"I have other examples."

"Such as?"

"You were tapping your toe during the show."

"It was a catchy tune!"

And the enthusiastic smile he wore at the end

of the performance? He'd probably say he was rewarding a job well done. "What made you pick that particular show in the first place, huh? Why not that hot hip-hop musical everyone's gushing about, if you were simply out to impress me? Don't tell me you couldn't have scored tickets to that if you'd wanted them. Instead, you picked a Christmas show, and not just any show. The Christmas Spectacular. Heck, even your choice of restaurant," she said, gesturing at the winter wonderland around them, "is Christmassy."

"I didn't exactly pluck the theme out of thin air. Since I arrived in Fryberg, you've made your attachment to Christmas quite clear. For crying out loud, your in-laws celebrate Christmas year-round."

"All the more reason for a person who hates holidays to show me something different," she replied. "But you didn't. You went full-on Christmas. What's more, you enjoyed everything as much as I did. And not—" she wagged her finger "—not simply because I was having fun."

James raised his glass to his lips. "How could

I not have a good time with such amazing company?"

Noelle blushed at the compliment. There was more though. She'd stolen enough looks during the day when he thought she wasn't looking. Saw the enjoyment on his face. Their adventure today had touched something inside him. The same sensitive part that was inspired to rent out the dining room.

She still couldn't believe he'd rented an entire rooftop for her. Talk about intimidating. She'd never been the focus of attention before, not by herself. Not without a Fryberg attached. The notion unsettled her.

Her thoughts were getting off track. "You're trying to distract me with compliments," she said, shaking her index finger. "No fair."

"*Au contraire*. I'm pretty sure all's fair," he replied.

"This isn't love or war."

"Yet."

He was joking. It was one date and, possibly, a few hours of intimacy. Neither of them expected anything more. Nevertheless, her stomach fluttered anyway. She reached for her wine, changed her mind, picked up her water and took a long drink to drown the sensation.

"Do you have any good memories of Christmas?" she asked, changing the subject.

He made a noise in his throat that sounded like an unformed groan. "We're back to talking about Christmas, are we?"

"We never left," she said. In spite of his efforts to dissuade her. "Surely, you must have some decent memories before your parents' marriage went sour." She was curious. There was a different James Hammond behind the cynicism, one that believed in moonlight dinners and making a woman feel like a princess, not for seduction purposes, but because he thought that's what a woman deserved. She wanted to get to know that James.

If she could coax him to talk.

He sat back and let out a long breath. "Easier asking for the Holy Grail. My parents never got along. Even before they separated, as soon as they spent extended time together, they would end up screaming and tossing dishes."

"Glass tumblers." She remembered.

"Exactly. Honestly, it's amazing they managed to have two kids." Frowning, he pushed his plate toward the center of the table. "There was this one Christmas. I was four. Maybe five. Hammond's was having some kind of event, for charity I think—I'm not sure. All I know is Santa was supposed to be there so my parents took Justin and me into Boston to see him. We had these matching wool coats and hats with flaps on them."

"Stylish," she said.

"Best-dressed kindergartener in the city."

His frown eased into a nostalgic-looking smile. "It was the first time I'd ever seen the Hammond's window displays. First time I remember seeing them anyway. We stood outside and watched them for hours. Although now that I say it out loud, it was probably more like ten minutes."

"Time has a way of slowing down when you're a kid."

"That it does," he said. "I read somewhere the passage of time changes based on how much of your lifetime you've lived. The author was very scientific. All I know is, on that afternoon, I could have watched those window displays forever."

He chuckled. "In one of the windows, a bunch of animals had broken into Santa's workshop. There was this squirrel inside a pot on one of the shelves that kept popping up. Every time he did, Justin would squeal and start laughing. Every time," he repeated. "Like it was the first time." And he rolled his eyes the way Noelle imagined his four-year-old self had. The image made her heart turn over.

"But you knew better," she teased.

"Totally. Who cared about some stupid squirrel when there was a polar bear looking in the window? At least the squirrel was inside the workshop. The bear was obviously in the store. What if he ate Santa Claus?"

"Obviously."

"Hey, don't laugh. Polar bears can be ruthless creatures."

"I'm not laughing." Not much anyway. His exaggerated earnestness made staying completely serious impossible. She could picture the moment in her head. Little James, his eyes wide and serious, worried about Santa's safety. "What did you do?"

"I thought we should call the police so they could tranquilize him, but my father assured me that all the polar bears at the North Pole were Santa's friends, and if there was one in the store, he was probably Santa's pet. Like a puppy."

"And that worked?"

His gaze dropped to the table. "Yeah, it did. If my father said the polar bear was a pet, then I believed him. Funny how at that age, you believe everything your parents tell you."

"The voice of definitive authority," Noelle said.

"I guess," he replied. "Anyway, we saw Santa, he told me the bear was taking a nap when I asked, and that Christmas I found a stuffed polar bear in my stocking. Damn thing sat on my bureau until junior high school."

When his world fell apart.

Afraid he'd come to the same conclusion, she reached across the table and took his hand. He responded with a smile and a fan of his thumb across her skin.

"I bet you were an adorable little boy. Protecting Santa Claus from danger."

"More like worried I wouldn't get presents. I'd have gladly sacrificed Justin if it meant finding a race car set under the tree."

"Did you?"

"You know, I don't remember."

But he remembered the window displays, and the polar bear toy, and his childhood wonder.

"You know," she said, "they say Christmas brings out the child in people. That's why adults go so gung ho for the holiday."

"Oh, really?" He entwined their fingers. "In your case, I'd say that's definitely true."

"It is for you as well. Seriously," she said when he rolled his eyes. "You can talk about hating Christmas all you like, but today's little adventure proves that little boy who watched the window displays is in there, way down deep."

"That little boy also pulled off Santa's beard."

He was so determined to pretend he didn't have a soft side. "Fine, be that way," she told him. "I know better. Thou protest too much."

"I beg your pardon?"

"You heard me," she said, reaching for her glass. "You may act all cynical and talk about greeting card fantasies, but you don't one hundred percent believe it. If you did, you'd convince your father to redo the Boston store, tourist attraction or no. We both know you could do so successfully." Instead, he doubled down on the Christmas fantasy every year. The reason hadn't hit her until tonight, as she looked around the winter wonderland he'd rented.

He may never have had a greeting card family Christmas, but he wanted one. Over the years, whenever she'd looked at photos of the Boston store, she had sensed a secondary emotion hovering behind the nostalgia and charm, but she could never give the feeling a name. Until tonight. Like a completed jigsaw, now that the pieces had fallen in place, she could recognize the emotion clear as day. It was longing.

Hope.

That was why James authorized the window displays every year, and why he kept the Boston store unchanged despite his insistence they focus on the future. The Boston store wasn't selling a greeting card fantasy to tourists. It represented *his* Christmas fantasy.

How on earth had she missed it? If anyone knew what it was like to hope on Christmas… She'd bet he didn't even realize what he was doing.

"You're staring," James said.

"Am I?" Lost in thought, she hadn't realized. "I didn't mean to stare. I was thinking how stubborn you are."

"Me, stubborn? Says the woman who refused to move a moose?"

"Elk, and that's different. Fryer is part of our great tradition. And at least I fought to protect something the town has had for years. You're going out of your way to avoid looking sensitive."

As expected, he rolled his eyes again. At least, there was a blush accompanying it this time. She was making progress. "You know," she said, sitting back in her chair. "There's nothing wrong in admitting a vulnerable side. Some people might even be impressed."

He laughed. "Some people being you."

"Maybe." She shrugged. Truthfully, she was already impressed. Probably too impressed, if she stopped to think about it.

She waited while he studied their hands, a smile playing on his lips. "I never should have told you I enjoy it when you challenge me," he said.

"Yeah, well, hindsight is always twenty-twenty," she teased before sobering. "What I'm trying to say—very badly, apparently—is that it's okay for you to let your guard down around me. That is, you don't have to feel awkward about showing…"

Thinking of all the ways he'd already opened up, she realized how foolish she sounded. Psychoanalyzing and advising him on his feelings. "Never mind. You don't need my encouragement."

Slipping her hand from his, she pushed her chair away from the table and started folding her napkin. "I wonder what time it is? We probably won't get back to Fryberg until after midnight."

"Once," James said.

"Once what?" She set her napkin on the table

and waited. James hadn't moved. His eyes remained on the spot where their hands had been.

"You wanted to know how often I bought out restaurants to impress women. The answer is once." He lifted his eyes. "Tonight."

Holy cow.

His answer rolling around her brain, Noelle stood up and walked to the window where, a few blocks away, the lights of Rockefeller Center created a glowing white canyon amid the buildings. "I was pretty sure you were joking about the whole rich-and-trying-to-seduce-you thing, but at the same time, I thought for sure you'd done stuff like this before."

She heard his chair scraping against the wood floor. A moment later, her back warmed with his presence. "Stuff?"

"You know… Sweeping a girl off her feet. Making her feel like Cinderella at the ball."

"Nope," he replied, mimicking the way she'd said the word earlier. "Only you."

She pressed a hand to her stomach to keep the quivers from spreading. "What makes me so special? If you don't mind my asking."

Silence greeted her question. The warmth disappeared from behind her, and then James was by her side, leaning against the chair rail. "I've been trying to answer that same question for two days," he said, "and damned if I know. All I know is you've had me acting out of character since Thanksgiving.

"Damn disconcerting too," he added under his breath.

"Most men would have answered a little more romantically," she said.

"I thought you knew by now that I'm not most men. Besides, you wanted me to drop my guard and be honest."

"Yes, I did," she replied, and James did not disappoint. What she hadn't expected was how enticing his honesty would be. Romantic words could be laughed off or discounted, but truth? Truth went right to your heart. Noelle liked that he didn't know why. Liked that his behavior frustrated him. That made her feel more special than any word ever could.

Suddenly, James wasn't close enough.

She moved left until they stood face-to-face,

hip to hip. "I can't explain why you get to me either."

There was heat in his eyes as he wrapped her in his arms. "Then we'll just have to be confused together."

CHAPTER TEN

"I KNOW WHAT'S topping my Christmas list this year."

Beneath Noelle's cheek, James's chest rumbled with his husky voice. She tucked herself tighter against his ribcage and let her fingertips ghost across his bare chest. "What's that?" she asked.

"A couple hundred more nights like this."

Sounded perfect. "You think Santa can fit them all in his sleigh?"

"He'll have to make them fit, because I won't settle for anything less. Wouldn't want to have to give him a bad online review. You know how he is about naughty and nice and all that."

"Sounds like someone gets silly when they're tired," she said, before planting a kiss on his skin. She liked silly. It was a side of him, she imagined, very few people got to see.

James rolled over and surrounded her in his embrace. They lay together like opposing spoons, with her head on his shoulder. "I'm not that tired," he said.

A yawn belied his words.

"All right, maybe a little. That was…"

"Amazing?" The word washed warm over her, causing her already boneless body to melt a little more.

"Mmm."

Noelle hadn't known. Sex with Kevin had been fine—she hadn't known anything else—but this… Her skin still hummed from being stroked. It was as if in touching her, James marked her inside and out, each caress and kiss seared into her skin like a brand.

The sensations went beyond physical though. She felt she'd woken from a long, unproductive sleep. When James sent her over the edge, he sent her to a place beyond her body. A place so high and bright, she swore she saw white. She'd wanted to float there forever.

And very nearly did.

James's fingers were tracing patterns along her arm. In her mind, she imagined them painting lines along her skin. To match the other marks he'd made.

"How about we fly to Boston in the morning, and lock ourselves in my apartment?" he suggested. "We can stay in bed until next year."

"We'd have to move though." Physical separation didn't seem possible at the moment. "Wouldn't it be easier to stay right here?"

"Nuh-uh. Boston's better." Sleep was turning his voice into a slur.

"Better than New York?"

"Better than anywhere. You'll see."

"I wouldn't say anywhere," she replied. "Fryberg's pretty special too, you know."

A soft snore stopped her from saying anything more.

So much for pillow talk. Shifting onto her elbow, Noelle used her new position to steal an uninterrupted look at the man beside her. Like she had on his first night in Fryberg, she marveled at James's beauty. The way all his features worked together to create the perfect face. Not perfect as in perfection, but perfect as in captivating. His cheekbones. His lashes. His parted lips. Leave it to him to make snoring seem attractive.

Awake, he looked older. There was a weight of the world behind his hazel eyes. When he slept, that weight faded, and hints of the boy he must have been leaked through. She would have liked to have known James as a boy. She would have told him he wasn't alone. She would have made him feel like he belonged, same way the Frybergs did her.

The Frybergs.

Her heart started to race. What had she done? She'd slept with another man. No, not slept with, *connected* with. What happened between her and James went beyond sex. Her entire love life with Kevin paled in comparison.

She felt awful just thinking the words. But they were the truth. She didn't feel guilty for sleeping with James; if anything, she felt guilty for enjoying the experience. She wanted to curl up in his arms and when James woke up, make love with him again. For crying out loud, she couldn't even use the word *sex*, because it was too inadequate a word.

"Damn you," she whispered. Why couldn't he remain the annoyingly dislikable boss she'd met on Wednesday morning? Why'd he have to get all romantic and vulnerable? Someone she could fall for?

If she hadn't fallen for him already.

She sat up, causing James's arm to slip away. He grumbled softly before rearranging himself, his head coming to rest on her hip while his arm wrapped around her thigh.

Reflexively, her fingers started combing his hair. The bump under his stitches was beginning to recede, she noticed. That was a good sign. She combed around the unruly patch where the hair and stitches met and tried to ignore the way her heart was expanding.

She *was* falling for him. Hard. And he was falling for her—there was no way that tonight had been one-sided. No, they might be at the very beginning, but the emotions in this bed had the potential to become something very real and special. It was the last thing she'd expected, but there it was.

The air in the room was suddenly getting close.

Her lungs wouldn't fill. She tried breathing in as hard as she could, but it was as if the air wouldn't flow past her lips.

Fresh air. That's what she needed. To clear her head so she could think.

Slipping out from beneath the covers, she padded toward the window only to find it couldn't open. Apparently New Yorkers didn't believe in throwing up the sash like they did in Fryberg. Very well, she'd risk a walk. A couple of moments of fumbling in the dark later, she was dressed and slipping out the door.

The brightness caught her off guard. She was used to seeing stars after midnight, not soft drink billboards and scrolling news feeds. After the soft lighting of their hotel room, the contrast hurt her eyes. Noelle leaned against the icy marble, and inhaled. The air was cold and sour smelling. A mixture of body odor and exhaust. A few blocks away, a trio of young women giggled their way toward her. They looked cold with their short jackets and exposed legs. Just looking at them made Noelle stuff her hands deeper into her pockets.

If she were smart, she'd turn around and head back inside.

Back to James. No sooner did she think his name than her heart started racing again.

She was scared. She didn't want to be falling in love.

Was that what was happening? James certainly was someone she *could* love. Being with him these past two days, she'd felt like a different person. Not Kevin Fryberg's widow or the infamous Manger Baby, but like *herself.* For the first time that she could remember, she hadn't felt grateful for the attention. Maybe it was because they shared similar pasts, but when she was with James, she felt worthy. As though she was the gift.

She should be thrilled by the feeling. Why then was she standing panicked and shivering on a New York sidewalk?

"Like I would even be interested in the loser... Not that desperate... She's such a skank!" The female trio was crossing the street, talking simultaneously. They had their arms linked. Holding each other up, no doubt, since they swayed back and forth as they walked. A blonde on the far end looked to be swaying more than the others, and as they got closer, Noelle realized it was because she was bouncing to a song she was singing. Her movement caused the middle one to pitch forward and stumble.

"What are you looking at?" she slurred as they stumbled past.

Noelle blinked. "Nothing," she replied, but the trio had already passed on, the blonde turning the air blue as she heaved a string of crude obscenities in her direction. Half the words, Noelle had never heard a person actually say out loud. Feeling like she'd been punched, she tried to flatten herself farther against the building.

Something fuzzy brushed her ankle.

Oh, God, a rat! Noelle shrieked and jumped forward. City rats were rabid, weren't they? She whipped her head back and forth to see which direction the horrid creature went.

Except it wasn't a rat at all. It was a hand. A rattily gloved hand that had slipped free of a dark lump. In her distraction, she hadn't noticed the body rolled up tight against the building. The person moaned and rolled over to reveal a weathered dirty face partially covered by a winter hat. White eyes stared out at her in the darkness as he moaned again. Despite the late hour, there was enough light to see his lips moving. He was trying to tell her something.

Swallowing in nerves, she moved closer and crouched down so she could hear. As she did, she realized he was the source of the sour smell from earlier. Body odor and alcohol swamped her nostrils.

"Do you need something?" she asked, opening her pocketbook. She only had a few dollars on her, but if it would help…

The vulgar name he called her brought her up short.

Her head snapped back. "Wh-What?"

"You ain't takin' my vent. Get your own fraking spot. I ain't sharin' my heat with nobody."

The rant pushed her backward. Stumbling, she sat down hard. Tears sprang to her eyes from the impact, but she ignored them as she pushed herself to her feet. The homeless man was waving her off now as well, his voice growing loud and angry.

"I'm—I'm…sorry. I'm leaving right now." Dropping a handful of bills by his hand—which he snatched while continuing to swear at her— she scurried backward, afraid to turn around until she'd put a safe distance between them. She traveled no more than a yard or two when her foot slipped off the curb. A horn blared. A taxicab had stopped in the intersection.

"Hey, lady. Watch where you're going!"

Nodding, she hurried across the street, and didn't stop until she reached a sign indicating an all-night coffee shop. There was a waitress behind the counter playing with her phone. She looked up when Noelle entered, and pointed to an empty stool.

"Counter service only," she said, before going back to her phone.

Noelle took a seat between two bulky customers, both of whom glared at her desire for space. "Sorry," she heard herself murmur again.

"Coffee?" the waitress asked.

Not really, but Noelle was too shy to ask for anything else. "Yes, please," she replied.

The waitress slapped down a mug and a bowl

of plastic creamers. Noelle shivered and wrapped her hands around the cup. Everything was so cold all of a sudden. Cold and angry. This was nothing like the New York James had shown her. But then, he'd gone out of his way to show her only the magical parts. What she was seeing now was the other New York, the part that dwelt beneath the twinkling lights and Christmas trees.

The realistic part, James would say. She'd been trying to keep this part of the world at bay since foster care.

What if falling in love with James was like that?

Sure, everything seemed wonderful now, but what if being with him was like New York and what looked beautiful at the beginning turned out to be filled with garish lights and cold, burnt coffee? It had happened before with Kevin. Hadn't she convinced herself he was the love of her life? What if she woke up one morning and discovered she'd made another mistake? Where would she be then? *Who* would she be then? She wouldn't be a Fryberg, not after betraying Kevin's memory, and they were the only family she'd ever had.

She'd be alone again. Back to the days when

she was an outsider at the dinner table. Present but not truly belonging.

Manger Baby.

Suddenly, she felt very small and alone. Add in a few schoolyard taunts and she'd be ten years old again. Lost and longing for a family to call her own.

"You want anything else?" a voice asked.

Noelle looked up to find the waitress looking in her direction. *Yeah*, she thought, *I could use a hug.* "No thanks. I'm good."

If she were home, Belinda would hug her. Like her son, she hugged fiercely. When a Fryberg encircled you in their arms, nothing in the world could harm you.

You come visit us anytime you want, Noelle. Any friend of Kevin's is a friend of ours.

Tears sprang to her eyes as Noelle remembered that wonderful first afternoon at Kevin's house. Had Mr. Lowestein known what he was giving her when he assigned Kevin as her lab partner? One step over the threshold and she had the family she'd always wanted.

And now, Kevin and Ned were dead. Belinda

was moving. The store had changed hands. Everything she cared about and deemed important was slipping out of her fingers. If she lost Belinda's love along with everything else...

She couldn't lose it. She couldn't go back to being alone. She needed...

Needed...

"I need to go home."

Her announcement fell on deaf ears, but it didn't matter. Noelle knew what she had to do. With any luck, James would understand.

Slapping a five-dollar bill on the counter, she headed outside.

James woke up to the sound of his cell phone buzzing. At first he tried ignoring the noise by putting the pillow over his head, but no sooner did the call stop, than the phone started buzzing again.

"Whoever it is, they're fired," he groaned. Leaning over the side of the bed, he groped along the floor until he found his jacket and dug the phone from the breast pocket. The name on the call screen made his shoulders stiffen.

"It's the crack of dawn," he said. "Is something wrong?"

"It's early afternoon here," his father replied. "You're usually up this hour."

"I slept in." Sort of. Raising himself on his elbows, he looked to the other side of the bed, only to frown at the empty sheets. Noelle must have slipped into the bathroom. "Is everything all right?" he asked. "You don't usually call on Sunday mornings."

"Shouldn't I be asking you that question?" Jackson said in return. "Carli said there was an..." He cleared his throat. "An issue at the Fryberg store the other day."

How like Jackson to call his being struck in the head an "issue." "I had a minor accident is all," he said.

"So everything is all right there?"

"Everything is fine." He told his father he had the Fryberg deal under control. A bump on the head wouldn't change anything.

Jackson cleared his throat again. "I'm glad to hear it. Carli didn't have too many details so I wanted to make certain myself. When I had trouble connecting with you, I thought perhaps there had been a problem."

"No," James said. "No problems. I've just been very busy here, and with the time change and all…"

"Right. Right. I'm glad…things…are going smoothly." There was a pause on the other end of the line, like his father was reading something. Multitasking and distraction were par for the course with Jackson. "When do you think you'll be back in Boston?"

"I'm not sure." The irony of his answer made him smile. Three days ago, he'd been champing at the bit to leave. "There are some…developments I want to look into."

"Developments?"

"Nothing problematic, I assure you."

On the contrary. If last night was any indication, he was on the cusp of something very significant. Noelle made him feel… He couldn't think of how to articulate his feelings. Special? Important? Neither word fit. How did he describe his heart suddenly feeling a hundred times larger?

"You'll keep me advised though, won't you?

I want to know if there are any complications," his father said. "Doesn't matter if they are big or small. I'd prefer you not go silent again."

"Of course. I didn't mean to give you cause for concern."

"James, I'm always…" There was another pause. A longer one this time.

James couldn't help the way his breath caught. If he didn't know better, he'd say his father had been worried. "You're what?" he asked.

"I've decided to stop in Copenhagen before I head home."

"Oh." That wasn't what he was going to say. He looked down at the wrinkles on the sheets beneath him. Like tiny white rivers leading to Noelle's side.

Maybe it isn't all about business, she'd said. *You still have hope.*

What the hell. It was worth a try. "Hey, Dad?" The word felt odd on his tongue from lack of use. "Do you remember going into Boston to see the window displays?"

"I'm afraid you're going to have to be more specific. I examine the window displays every year."

"This was with me and Justin and…and Mom. Back when we were…" A family. "We went to see Santa Claus."

"I remember your mother hated those trips. She only went because Justin insisted. Why?"

So much for his wonderful family memory. "I was thinking about repeating one of the designs next year. Vintage is very trendy right now."

"But will it be in fashion next year, that's the question," his father replied. "Trends fall out of favor quickly these days."

As did memories. "It was just a thought."

"Well, you know my position on those displays. They outlived their expenditure long ago. I'll be back by the middle of the week. Why don't we connect then? Over dinner, perhaps."

"Okay," James said. With any luck he would have to cancel to take a certain sexy little elf sightseeing in Boston. "Have a safe trip."

"You too, James."

He let the phone drop to the floor. Stupid, his feeling kicked in the gut over one comment. Wasn't like his father was revealing some kind of family secret. At least Noelle wanted him. The way he felt with her trumped anything—every-thing—else. Simply thinking her name chased his dark thoughts away.

Damn, but he was falling hard for her.

He stretched his arm to pull her close, only to remember when he struck bare sheets that she was still in the bathroom. "You can come out of hiding! I'm off the phone," he called with a smile. It was sweet that she wanted to give him privacy.

When she didn't respond, he flipped over on his back. "Noelle? Babe? You okay?"

The bathroom door was wide open.

What the hell? Jumping from the bed, he rushed across the room and slapped on the bathroom light. The room was empty. He knew it would be empty. He'd just hoped…

That was the problem with hope. It always ended with a sucker punch.

Noelle was gone. While he'd been dreaming of waking up beside her, she'd gotten dressed and left.

Maybe she went to get coffee, a small, desperate voice in his head said. He angrily shoved the idea away before it could take hold. He didn't want to entertain possibilities, didn't want *hope*. His fingers squeezed the towel rod, his body trembling with the desire to rip it from the wall. He could still see the way she looked at him in the restaurant. Like she cared.

Dammit. He smashed a fist on the marble vanity, roaring through gritted teeth at the pain. Dammit, dammit, dammit! Why couldn't she have stayed a mildly attractive employee? No, she had to crawl under his skin and make him start to believe the damn greeting card was possible? He thought yesterday had been as mind-blowing for her as it had for him. He thought they were starting something here. He thought…

He thought she cared.

Joke was on him, wasn't it? Like he could compete with her dead war hero of a husband. For crying out loud, his own parents didn't want him; what made him think Noelle would?

If only she hadn't been so damn special.

Forget it. Taking a deep breath, James pushed the rage down as deep as possible. He tucked it away along with the crazy dream he'd had of sharing the holidays with Noelle.

Turned out, he'd been right all along. Things like family and holiday cheer, hope, love—they were pipe dreams. Marketing concepts designed to manipulate emotions and sell products. They didn't really exist. At least not for him.

Lesson learned.

CHAPTER ELEVEN

IF NOELLE HEARD the guy on the sound system sing about Santa coming to town one more time, she was going to scream. The song, part of a continual loop in the store, had been playing for the past three days. Usually, she embraced Christmas carols, but she hadn't slept well since returning from New York, and the lack of sleep had left her with a throbbing knot at the back of her head. Like she'd been smacked in the head by a drone.

If only she could be so lucky. A smack to the head and temporary amnesia sounded pretty good about now. Anything would, if it meant whipping out Saturday's memories. She had her own continual loop of sounds and images tormenting her. Every night when she tried to sleep, they repeated in her head. James smiling. James propped on his elbows above her. James raining kisses on her skin. Over and over, the memories repeated until she ended up clutching a pillow to her aching insides while she waited for the clock to signal morning.

Not that daytime was all that much better. If she drove past the Christmas market, she thought of James. If she visited Santa's workshop, she thought of James. If she walked past her living room sofa...

For goodness' sake, they'd known each other four days! Their relationship didn't warrant this kind of obsession. Yet, here she was obsessing.

Her guilty conscience didn't help. She should have gone back to the hotel and explained in person, but she'd been so freaked out by what she was feeling that she was halfway home before she'd thought things through. By then, embarrassment had kicked in, and the best she could do was a text reading *I'm sorry.* As far as regrets went, it was the stupidest, most immature thing she'd ever done.

Her gaze drifted to her telephone. It wasn't too late. She could still call and explain. What would she say? *Sorry I ran out on you, but I liked you so much I freaked?* While true, she doubted it would make a difference. When push came to shove, it was still only one night—one fantastical, mind-blowing, life-altering night—but one night all the same. And there was still the chance she'd read the situation wrong. After all, she was assuming he felt the same way. For all she knew, the way she felt after they'd made love was commonplace for James and his talk of showing her Boston was nothing more than pillow-talk promises. It had only been a few days, but he might have already moved on, and calling would simply make her look foolish.

A knock sounded on her door. Looking up, she saw Todd standing in the doorway. His arms were folded, and he wore a frown. "You okay?" he asked.

"Fine," she replied, pretending to shuffle some papers. "What can I do for you?"

"I was wondering if you've read the email from the Boston office yet."

Boston office meaning James. Her stomach did a little bounce. "No. What did it say?"

"Hammond sent a list of recommendations for how we can streamline operations and improve traffic flow in the store. Looks like he took a lot of mental notes during his tour last week. Pretty impressive for a guy with stitches in his head."

"Streamlining is his thing," she replied. Along with renting out restaurants and nipping at shoulders, she thought, fighting a blush.

Either she succeeded or Todd was too polite to say anything. "Some of his changes we won't be able to implement until after the holidays, but a few we can put in place now. Why don't you read the list and then you and I can talk?"

"Sure thing." Reaching for her mouse, she clicked on the email icon and brought up her inbox on the screen. "Has Belinda seen the list? What did she say?"

"Nothing. She officially stepped away from operations on Monday afternoon, remember?"

"Sorry. I forgot." This time, Noelle did blush.

"Totally understand," Todd replied. "It's going to take some getting used to, not thinking of her as being in charge."

Or being around, thought Noelle. The first thing her mother-in-law mentioned after Noelle's return on Sunday was that she planned to leave for Florida right after Christmas and not return until mid-April. So in the end, Noelle didn't have James or her family.

Todd cleared his throat. "You sure you're okay? You seem a little spacey."

"Sorry," she apologized again. "I was scanning the memo."

He nodded, even though the expression on his face said he didn't believe her for a second. "Soon as you've gone through it, come find me. I'm looking forward to hearing your thoughts. Especially about point number five."

Point number five, huh? She clicked open the email. Turned out, it wasn't from James after all, but rather a Carli Tynan. The suggestions were all James, however. She recognized the first two as ones he'd made during the tour. Quickly she scanned down to point five.

Remove the Elk statue from the rear of the store. In addition to taking up a large amount of space, the crowd that gathers around it impacts other shoppers' ability to maneuver in the aisles. Recommend statue be placed either outside on the grounds or in storage.

That rat! He'd promised Fryer would stay.

This was clearly revenge for her walking out. Completely unacceptable. It was one thing for him to be angry with her, but he had no business taking his anger out on a poor innocent elk. Fryer hadn't done a thing except uphold tradition.

Retrieving the Boston number from the bottom of the email, she picked up her phone and dialed.

"I want to talk to James Hammond," she snapped when the receptionist answered. There'd be plenty of time to regret her rudeness later. "Tell him Noelle Fryberg is on the phone, and that it's important."

Apparently, there was a part of her that didn't expect him to answer, because she nearly dropped the phone when James's voice drawled in her ear. "I'm in the middle of a meeting."

Nevertheless, he took her call. She might have taken that as a hopeful sign, if not for his chillingly businesslike voice.

She got straight to the point. "Fryer," she said. "Carli sent out the memo."

"She sent it out, all right. What are you doing

removing Fryer? We agreed he was a popular attraction, and deserved to stay."

"I changed my mind," James replied. "I had some time to think on my flight alone back to Boston and decided it wasn't a good idea. There's enough chaos in that store without teenagers blocking the aisles and taking selfies."

"On Friday you called that chaos organized."

"My perspective changed."

Noelle didn't think she'd ever heard his voice so emotionless, not even on his first day in Fryberg. He sounded like the warmth had been sucked out of him and it was her fault.

She grew sick to her stomach. "I'm sorry about the other night."

"I know. I received your text."

She winced. "I know I shouldn't have run out the way I did."

"Forget it, Noelle. I already have."

"You—you have?" Of course he had. Hadn't he said at the restaurant that he was a rich man trying to seduce her? She was the one who'd gone and attached deeper meaning to his behavior.

Maybe all the importance had been in her head. "But Fryer…"

"Business, Noelle. The store is a Hammond's property now. It seemed silly to wax nostalgic about the previous ownership." She could hear him shifting in his chair and pictured him sitting straight and stiff behind his desk. "Besides, I'm taking the chain in a different direction after the first of the year. Your elk clashes with the new brand."

"But we agreed," Noelle said. The protest came out a whine. Worst of all, it wasn't Fryer she cared about. It was the chill in his voice. So cold and detached. She wanted the voice that scorched her skin.

"Disappointment's part of life."

Ouch. Then again, what did she expect his attitude would be? Relief? He was angry, and Noelle deserved every ounce of wrath thrown her way.

"James—" *I'm sorry.*

Too late. He'd hung up.

Noelle let the receiver slip from her fingers. What had she done? Handled the whole situation like a child, that's what. One-night stand or not, James deserved a proper goodbye.

Everything was messed up.

"Argh!" Squeezing her eyes shut, she ground the heels of her palms into her lids. "What a freaking idiot."

"Little harsh, don't you think?" she heard Belinda ask. "I'm sure whoever you're talking about isn't that stupid."

The blurry image of her mother-in-law carrying a newspaper walked into the office. She was dressed in her off-duty clothes—jeans and a soft hand-knit sweater—and looked so much like the day they first met, that Noelle immediately jumped up and ran into her arms. Immediately, Belinda's arms went around her in a bear grip more comforting than she deserved. Noelle's shoulders started to shake.

"Whoa, what's this all about?" Belinda asked. "Are you crying?"

"I c-can't help it." Noelle gulped between sobs. The safer she felt, the more she cried.

"Come now, I'm sure it's not that bad."

Did she want to bet? Sniffing back her tears,

Noelle let herself catch her breath before speaking. "Fryer's gone," she said, sniffing again. "The Boston office wants him put in storage." And it was all her fault because she'd been a childish coward.

"Don't tell me all these tears are because of a battered old elk," Belinda said.

She stepped back and looked Noelle in the eye. "I know you're fond of tradition, sweetheart, but he's only an old statue. I tried to convince Ned to get rid of him for years. Thing takes up way too much space on the floor."

Great. In addition to dashing out on James, she'd been protecting a tradition no one else wanted.

How fitting.

"Then I guess you've finally gotten your wish." Backing out of her mother-in-law's embrace, Noelle turned back to her desk. "If I'd known you didn't care, I wouldn't have put up a fight."

"Don't be silly," Belinda said. "Of course you would have. You'll fight for every tradition. It's who you are. But something tells me all these tears aren't for our soon-to-be-departed mascot. Something's been bothering you all week."

"That obvious, is it?"

"Thirty seconds ago you were sobbing on my sweater. A billboard would be less obvious. What's wrong?"

Where to start? "It's complicated."

"Is it my retiring? I know my leaving for Florida is happening quickly."

"The business is only part of the problem," Noelle replied.

"I see." She wore Kevin's same skeptical expression as she folded her arms. "What's the other part?"

Shame burned in Noelle's stomach. Thinking her mistakes were bad enough, but speaking them aloud?

"I messed up," she said. "I did something really, really stupid."

"Oh, sweetheart." The older woman stepped up and rested a hand on Noelle's shoulder. "I'm sure you're exaggerating. Todd would have told me if it was super serious."

"Todd doesn't know, and worse, it's too late to fix things."

"You don't know that, sweetheart. Nothing is so horrible it can't be repaired."

"Not this time," Noelle replied, turning around. Taking a deep breath, she relayed what had happened in New York.

"Well," Belinda said when she finished, "that explains why James mysteriously cancelled our Monday meeting *and* why you were acting so strangely when you came by the house on Sunday afternoon. Why on earth would you run off and leave him like that?"

"Because I freaked out." She rubbed her forehead, the pain from the back of her head having decided to relocate there. "The way he made me feel. The emotions. They were too overwhelming. I've never felt like that before."

"Not even with Kevin?"

Noelle froze. Here she thought she couldn't mess up any further. "Kevin was... That is, I loved Kevin..."

"It's all right," Belinda said. "I know what you meant."

"Y-you do?"

"You and Kevin were practically babies when

you started dating. Only natural the grown-up you would feel things a little differently.

"Maybe…" Her mother-in-law's smile was indulgent as she cupped Noelle's cheek. "Maybe even a little stronger."

How did she earn such a wonderful person in her life?

"You have to know, I loved Kevin," Noelle replied. "I wanted to spend the rest of my life with him." Who knows how things would have worked out between them if he'd returned? They'd already had a strong foundation. Passion might have blossomed eventually as well.

"No matter what, he'll always own a big piece of my heart."

Belinda smiled down at her. "I know, sweetheart. Now, the question is—does James Hammond own any of that heart? Are you in love with him?"

Was she? Noelle shook her head. "We've only known each other four days." Far too soon to fall head over heels. "But…" She thought about how her heart felt fuller when he walked into a room.

"But you could see yourself falling in love with him someday," Belinda finished for her.

"Yes." Very much so, Noelle thought as she looked to the ground. She had the sinking feeling she was halfway in love now. Not that it mattered given her foolish behavior. "I'm sorry."

"Don't be ridiculous," Belinda replied. She forced Noelle to look up. "You never have to apologize for falling in love with someone else."

"But Kevin…"

"Kevin would want you to move on. So would Ned and I. You're much too young to spend your life alone."

Right, because Belinda was leaving. The reminder she would soon be alone in Fryberg only made the hollow feeling in Noelle's chest grow larger. "What if I'm wrong?" she asked. "What if James isn't as awesome as I think?"

"Then you try again," Belinda told her. "Relationships don't come with guarantees. Some work. Some don't."

"Yeah, but if I choose him, and we don't make it, then I'll be alone again." Her eyes had lost the battle and teared up again. One dripped down her cheek onto Belinda's fingers. "You're the only family I've ever had. I don't know what I'd do without you."

"My goodness, is that what you're scared of? Losing your family?"

She didn't see how she could move on and keep them. "I'm only family because I married Kevin. If I move on, I won't belong anymore."

"What are you talking about? Of course you'll belong. Don't you realize that with Kevin gone, I need you more than ever?"

Before she could say another word, Noelle found herself back in Belinda's embrace. Her mother-in-law squeezed her tight. "You, Noelle Fryberg, have always been more than Kevin's wife," she said. "I love you like a daughter, and that's never going to change, whether you fall in love with James Hammond or a hundred different men. Family is forever, and you..."

She kissed Noelle's forehead. "You are my family. Got that?"

Noelle tried to keep her jaw from trembling as she nodded. What a fool she was. So busy being grateful for Belinda and Ned's affections, she couldn't see that when it came to Belinda, family wasn't an either-or proposition. Her heart was large enough to accommodate everyone. Take Thanksgiving and the mishmash of characters who joined every year. Todd, Jake from the mail room, Nadifa from sales. None of them blood related and yet all of them embraced like they were.

When she thought about it, Belinda had pulled Noelle into that welcoming web the day Kevin brought her home. She didn't inherit a family *because* she dated Kevin; dating Kevin was an added bonus. Chances are she would have been enfolded into the Thanksgiving Day group regardless. After all, the only qualification was being alone at the holidays.

"Your family was—is—the greatest gift I could ever ask for," she told Belinda. "Being a Fryberg was a dream come true. It was all I ever wanted."

By now Belinda's eyes were shining too. "Oh, sweetheart, you're my dream come true too. Don't get me wrong, I loved Kevin, but I always wanted a daughter to keep the family traditions alive."

Offering a smile, the older woman bent down and kissed Noelle on the forehead. "I never imagined I'd end up with a daughter who's more Fry-berg than anyone with actual Fryberg blood."

They both laughed. "Does that mean I can still have Grandma Fryberg's recipe book?" Noelle asked, wiping her eyes.

"Absolutely. I'll even laminate the pages so you can pass the book along to your daughter.

"And you will have a daughter. Or daughter-in-law," Belinda added. Her smile faded and once again, her expression grew serious. "There's a whole world out there beyond this store and our family name. I fully expect you to build a happy life beyond Fryberg's. You deserve one."

"But I wouldn't have a life without Fryberg's," Noelle replied. Breaking out of her mother-in-law's grasp, she reached for the box of tissues on her desk. Her eyes and nose were runny with tears. "I can't imagine anything else."

"Really? Then why are you crying over James Hammond?"

All right, maybe Noelle could imagine a little more. The other night, in James's arms, she'd imagined all types of future. "Doesn't matter whether I'm crying over him or not," she said, blowing her nose. "He and I are finished."

"Are you certain?"

"Man said so himself."

Forget it, Noelle. I already have.

She blew her nose. "You should have heard his voice, Belinda." Remembering sent a chill down her spine. "I called him to discuss his email, and I might as well have been talking to a stranger."

A feeling of hopelessness washed over her. "I thought… That is, the whole reason I freaked out was because I thought we had some kind of special connection. Now I wonder if maybe I wasn't simply confusing good sex with affection and blew the weekend out of proportion."

Thankfully, Belinda chose to let the good sex comment slide. Hearing her thoughts out loud, however, made Noelle even more certain she was right, and had let the romanticism of Saturday night get the best of her. "Other than being angry with the way I took off, I wonder if James has even given me a second thought."

"I'm sure he has. He didn't strike me as someone who took…those kinds of encounters…lightly."

"Me either," Noelle replied. "He certainly sounded businesslike enough today though. Talking about the company's new direction and all."

"New direction?"

"Uh-huh. Based on the points in his email, I'd say he's back to focusing on streamlining and internet sales." She could see it now. Today Fryer. Tomorrow the Christmas Castle.

"Hmm."

Noelle frowned. "What?"

"I'm not sure," Belinda replied. "Did you see today's business headlines?"

"No."

"I think you should. There's something very interesting in it." Her mother-in-law retrieved the newspaper she'd dropped on the desk during their talk. It was folded in thirds, to highlight the headline on the weekly marketing column. Noelle's heart sank as she read.

Hammond's to discontinue iconic window displays.

The article below quoted James as saying he wanted to take the chain in a "new direction" and build a store for the next generation.

"'It's time Hammond's let go of the past,'" she read. "'We can't bring the past back, no matter how badly we may want to.'" It was a harsh-sounding quote, one she imagined marketing hadn't wanted to use.

"When I read the article this morning, something didn't hit me as right. Still doesn't, although I can't put my finger on what."

Noelle stared at the headline.

All week she'd been downplaying Saturday night to ease the giant ache in her chest, but her efforts hadn't worked. There were too many reminders in the Christmas music and lights. She wanted the holiday to go away so she could breathe again. She who held Christmas in her heart fifty-two weeks a year.

But ending the window displays? They represented the one decent family memory he had. It was why he kept them going year after year, regardless of the cost. Because there was a part of him, the ghost of that little boy, that wanted to believe family meant something. That he meant something to his family. Before his mother's midnight departure convinced him otherwise.

No. Noelle's heart seized. Dropping the newspaper, she stumbled toward a chair. The room had become a tunnel, a narrow dark tube with black all around.

"Are you all right?" she heard Belinda ask from far away. "Is something wrong? What is it?"

No. Yes. Everything. The answers flew through her head as her realization became clear.

She'd disappeared in the middle of the night without a word just like his mother. He'd spent the day revealing himself, at her urging, and she'd let her cowardice trample that vulnerability. In doing so, she solidified all of James's fears.

That was why he was closing the window displays. Not because he wanted to take the chain in a new direction—though he would and do so brilliantly—but because that little boy no longer believed in his own memory. James had retreated, quit, waved the white flag in defeat.

He had given up hope, and it was her fault.

It wasn't right. Someone needed to tell him he had too much sweetness and light inside him to hide behind profits and modern retail. Someone had to show him he was special.

Lovable.

Not someone. Her. Noelle needed to fix the horrible wrong she had done to him. And not by text or by phone either. In person.

"I need to go to Boston," she told Belinda. "As soon as possible."

She may have thrown away her chance to be with him, but Noelle would be damned if she cost him Christmas.

"Why are you still wearing your coat?" Jackson asked, as he slipped into his seat. As usual, he was dressed impeccably in a suit from his London tailor.

"I'm cold," James replied. "This table picks up a draft from the front door."

He and his father were meeting for a business lunch in the bistro across from Hammond's. Outside, Copley Square bustled with Christmas shoppers, many of who stopped to watch the Hammond's displays. In fact, there was a crowd of preschoolers clumped in front of them that very moment, watching the elves make mischief in Santa's kitchen. Why they were standing out in such blasted cold was beyond him. A shiver passed through him, and he looked away.

"If you're uncomfortable, we can move," Jackson said.

"That won't be necessary. I'll warm up soon enough." He hoped. He'd been chilled to the bone for days. At home, he'd cranked both his gas fireplace and the thermostat, and slept with an extra comforter. It was going to be a long winter, at this rate.

Maybe if he found someone to warm him up? He dismissed the idea as quickly as it appeared. Female company didn't appeal to him right now.

Meanwhile, for some reason, his father refused to let the subject drop. After the waiter took their orders, he laid his napkin on his lap and leaned forward. "Are you sure it's temperature-related and not something to do with the 'issue' you had in Fryberg?"

"I'm sure." Other than a minor case of temporary insanity, his "issue" had been side-effect-free. "A cup of hot coffee and I'll be fine."

Jackson stared at him for a beat or two. "If you say so," he said finally, before reaching for his water glass. "I saw the article in the *Business Journal* today about the window displays. I have to say I didn't think you would ever agree to eliminate them."

"What can I say? Even I couldn't ignore the numbers."

"I'm glad you finally came around. Although it would have been nice if you'd alerted me to your decision. I realize you handle these kinds of day-to-day operations, but..."

"You were in Copenhagen," James interrupted. "And I wanted to make the announcement early enough to take advantage of the entire Christmas season. I didn't mean to blindside you."

"*Surprise* is a better word."

James returned his father's flat smile and sipped his coffee. "Marketing tells me we're getting quite a bit of local press attention from the announcement. This could turn into a public relations bonus for us."

"That reminds me," Jackson said, "you need to talk to whoever wrote the press release. They should have drafted a less caustic quote."

James had written the quote himself. Molly,

their communications assistant, had clearly wanted something else, but she hadn't argued.

Noelle would have. He suppressed a shiver. "Actually, I thought the quote went straight to the point."

"'We can't bring the past back, no matter how badly we may want to'?" Jackson quoted. "I would have preferred something a little less cynical."

"Why? It's true, isn't it?"

"Yes, but we're not in the business of selling truth, James—we sell toys."

"Don't worry. I've no intention of letting sales slide." Amazing how unaffected he was about the whole thing. Not too long ago, he would have argued the window displays brought in customers. But when he'd visited the store on Sunday afternoon and saw this year's intricate displays, he'd suddenly thought *Why bother?* All that money spent and what did it matter?

"The rest of the chain does quite well without window displays," James said, reaching for his coffee again. "Boston will too. A month from now, people won't remember what the display looked like."

"I could have told you that," Jackson replied.

The waiter arrived with their food. While he waited for the man to serve his soup, James let his eyes travel back to the crowd across the street. The preschoolers had been joined by several mothers with strollers. For a moment, he thought he saw a red-and-white knit hat mixed in the crowd and his pulse stuttered. His eyes were playing tricks on him. He hadn't thought about Noelle since he left New York—prolonged thought anyway—and he wasn't about to start.

Although yesterday's phone call nearly killed him. When the receptionist said her name, a tearing sensation had gripped his chest. The first intense feeling he'd had in days, it nearly knocked him to his knees. Then there was the way she'd lowered her voice to apologize. It took all his reserves, but thankfully he kept himself from breaking and asking why she left. No need to hear her excuse. He already knew.

The sound of his father clearing his throat drew back his attention.

"Are you certain you feel all right?" Jackson asked. "Perhaps you should see a specialist."

"I'm *fine*," he insisted.

"You say you're all right, but you're clearly not acting like yourself. You're difficult to reach. You're making sudden changes in company policy."

James let out a long sigh. "So this is about my not discussing the announcement with you beforehand." He knew this sudden interest in his health had to mean something.

"This has nothing to do with the announcement," Jackson said, killing that theory immediately. "I'm simply concerned about you."

"Why? You've never been before." The words came flying out before James realized what he was saying. They landed between them, causing his father to sit back, his features frozen in shock.

"You don't think I care?" Jackson said. He actually sounded stung.

What did he do now?

Aww, heck. Might as well put this bit of the past to rest too. "I'm not making an accusation," James said, holding up a hand. "I understand that you were stuck with me when Mom left and that put you in an awkward position."

His father stared at him. A long look similar to the ones he'd given James as a teenager. And like then, James had to fight the urge to tug at his collar.

Finally, Jackson put down his fork. "Are you suggesting that I was unhappy when your mother left you behind?"

Wasn't he? "I remember the look on your face when I came downstairs that morning and you definitely weren't expecting to see me. If anything," he added, looking down at his chowder, "you looked disappointed."

"That's because I was," Jackson replied. "For you." He let out a sigh. "Your mother was a very unpredictable woman. Doing one thing one day, and something else the next. She insisted that I encouraged your analytical side to spite her, and that I didn't understand what it took to raise a child. I had no idea she'd left you behind until you came downstairs that morning.

"She was right," he said, smoothing a wrinkle from the tablecloth. "I was completely unprepared."

Silence filled the table while his father paused

to sip his water and James struggled for what to say next. It was true; his mother had been high-strung. Hence the flying crystal. He remembered preferring the quiet of his father's study to being around her whirling dervish personality.

"I'm not…" Jackson took another drink. "I'm not a naturally affectionate person. Your mother complained all the time that I was too detached. Too stiff. It's how I am. Looking back, I can see how an impressionable teenager might miscon-strue my behavior.

"I can assure you, though," he added, "that at no time did I ever consider myself 'stuck' with you."

Slowly stirring his soup, James digested his fa-ther's confession. So he had been wanted after all. As far as family reconciliations went, the moment wouldn't win any prizes, but he got a tightness in his chest nonetheless. "Thank you," he said. "I appreciate you telling me."

For the first time in James's life, Jackson Ham-mond looked bashful. "You're welcome. Son."

By unspoken agreement, they spent the rest of the luncheon discussing business, a far more com-fortable subject. When they were finished, Jackson suggested they meet for lunch again the next week. "Or you could come by for dinner," he offered.

"Sure," James replied. If his father could try, then so could he. "Dinner would be great."

Jackson responded with the most awkward shoulder pat in history. Still it was a start.

Not that he would ever say so, but his father had terrible timing. Short as it was, their heart-to-heart killed the numbness he'd so carefully cultivated when Noelle left. Granted, he'd been cold, but with one or two exceptions, he'd been able to function without thinking about what a fool he'd been.

But then, Jackson decided to pat his shoulder, and the first thought that popped into his head was *Noelle was right*. Suddenly, the entire weekend was replaying in his head.

Telling his father he had an errand, James hung back on the sidewalk as Jackson entered the building. He needed to clear his head of the frustration his father's apology had unleashed. It felt like a giant fist shoving upward in his chest.

If he didn't push it back down, he was liable to scream out loud.

Why was he letting one tiny woman get to him so badly?

Dammit! He'd had one-night stands before. Some of them even told him to go to hell after they discovered they were nothing more than one-night stands. None of those experiences had ever turned into an existential crisis. His weekend with Noelle shouldn't have either, late-night escape or otherwise. Yet here he was, making long overdue peace with his father and wishing it was Noelle reaching out to him instead.

He never should have let her past his defenses. From the start, he knew nothing *real* could happen between them. Relationships didn't happen on his end of the bell curve. But then she'd hugged him, shifting around his insides and allowing things like hope and longing to rise to the surface. She'd made him believe their night together went deeper than sex. He hadn't just taken her in his arms; he'd shared his soul with her. Every touch, every kiss was his way of expressing the feelings she unlocked in him. Fool that he was, he'd actually started believing in Hammond's marketing pitch.

And now, thanks to his father's apology, those feelings threatened to return, this time to mock him. He didn't want to feel. He didn't want to hope anymore.

From here on in, it was about business. Profit and efficiency.

"Ooh, look, Andre! There's a monkey swinging in the lights. Do you see him?"

Lost in his thoughts, James didn't realize he'd joined the crowd in front of the window displays. Next to him, a young mother in a leather jacket stood holding a toddler. She had a second baby, bundled in pink bunting in a stroller beside her.

The woman pointed a manicured finger toward the window. "Look at him," she said. "He's trying to steal Santa's cookies."

The toddler, Andre presumably, had a frown on his pudgy puce-colored face. "Bad monkey," he said. "No cookies."

"You don't think he should take the cookies?" the mother asked, laughing as the toddler shook his head.

"Someone's taken the naughty list concept to heart," James caught himself saying.

"Let's hope he feels that way when he's ten," she replied. "You ready to see the next window, Dre?"

Watching the trio walk away, a pang struck James in the midsection as he realized Dre and his little sister wouldn't see the displays next year. Oh, well, at their age, they wouldn't even realize the loss. Most kids wouldn't. It was just James holding on to the memory.

Did his brother ever think about the window displays? Last time he saw Justin… When was the last time he'd seen him? The boat races maybe? Jackson had said something about his brother going to business school out west somewhere. James didn't even know what college his brother had attended. Or where he did his undergrad, for that matter. Like mother, like son, Justin had had little to do with them once he left. He'd apparently built quite a nice Hammond-free life and wasn't looking back.

James needed to do the same. It helped that at least Jackson had confessed he wasn't completely unwanted.

Just unwanted by his mother.

And by Noelle. Out of the corner of his eye, he saw another flash of red and white, causing the frustration to rise anew.

Four more weeks. Come January first, Christmas would be done, they would pack away the decorations, and he would be rid of any and all reminders of Fryberg. No more thoughts of blue eyes or snow-dotted lashes.

In the meantime, James had a business to run. The numbers at their Cape Cod store were especially troublesome and needed to be addressed.

Feeling his control return, he marched into the store.

His renewed focus lasted until he reached the top floor. There, he barely managed to round the corner to his office when a red-and-white cap stopped him in his tracks.

So much for blaming his imagination.

Noelle rose from her seat. "I need to talk with you," she said.

CHAPTER TWELVE

SHE LOOKED…BEAUTIFUL. The image of her lying in his arms flashed before him, and his body moved to take her in his arms. Catching himself, James clasped his hands behind his back.

"If you're here about that blasted elk there's nothing more to talk about," he said.

"I'm not here about Fryer," she said.

"Good. Then we have even less to talk about. If you'll excuse me…"

He tried to brush past her and head into his office, but she stepped in front of him. A five-foot-two roadblock. "I read about you canceling the window displays."

"And let me guess, you're worried how the new direction will affect your Christmas Castle." Why else would she fly halfway across the country instead of emailing? All roads led to Fryberg, didn't they?

"You could have saved yourself the airfare. Our plans for the castle haven't changed. Your family business will live to bring another year of Christmas cheer."

Again, he moved to his office and again, she blocked his path. "I'm not here about the castle either."

"Then why are you here?" he asked. It was taking all his effort to keep his voice crisp and businesslike. What he wanted was to growl through clenched teeth.

"Because I owe you an apology."

Seriously? James ignored how her answer made his heart give a little jump. Not again, he reminded himself. No more being fooled into believing emotions existed when they didn't.

"You wasted your airfare. I told you on the phone, the matter has already been forgotten."

This time, he managed to pass her and reach his office door.

"I know what you're doing." Noelle's voice rang through the waiting area.

Don't take the bait. Don't turn around.

"Is that so?" he replied, turning. "And what is that, exactly?"

"You're trying to kill Christmas."

Someone dropped a stapler. Out of the corner of his eye he saw his administrative assistant picking up several sheets of paper from the floor.

"You're being ridiculous." He couldn't kill Christmas if he tried. Damn holiday insisted on existing whether he wanted it to or not.

"Am I? I know what those displays meant to you. How much you loved them..."

His assistant dropped her stapler again.

He closed his eyes. "Noelle, this is neither the time nor the place for us to have this conversation."

"Fine," she replied. "When and where would you like to have it?"

"How about nowhere and never?"

"Nice try, but I flew across five states to talk to you so I can say what I have to say now or I can say it later, but I'm not leaving until I speak my piece."

He expected her to fold her arms after her speech, but instead, she looked up at him through her lashes, and added, "Please?" Her plea totally threw him a curveball. No way he could resist those cornflower eyes.

"Fine. We'll talk." Opening his office door, he motioned for her to step in first. "But take off that hat." No way was he rehashing Saturday night with her looking adorable.

Unfortunately, she looked more adorable with tousled hat hair. He went back to clasping his hands to keep from combing his fingers through it.

Nodding to one of the chairs, he walked around to the other side of his desk and sat down figuring a three-foot cherrywood barrier would keep him from doing something stupid.

"Okay, you've got the floor," he said. "What was so important that you had to fly all the way to Boston to say?"

"Aren't you going to take off your coat?"

"No. I'm cold." Although that status was rapidly changing, thanks to his heart rate. It had started racing the second he saw her. "Now what is it you wanted?"

"Why are you closing down the window displays?"

"Because they're a financial drain on the company."

"Funny how you didn't think so before," she replied coming toward the desk.

"Well, I saw them with a new perspective. I realized we were spending a lot of money trying to sell a concept that no longer resonated." Was she coming around to his side of the desk? "My decision shouldn't be a surprise," he said. "My feelings about this kind of kitschy Christmas marketing were hardly a secret."

She stopped at the desk corner. "You didn't think them so kitschy on Saturday night when you told me about the polar bear."

"That's because I was trying to charm you into bed. And it worked. At least for a little while," he added. If she was going to stand so close, he was going to wield sarcasm.

God, but he wished she'd back away. It was easier to be furious with her when he couldn't smell orange blossoms.

"It was wrong of me to run out like that," she said. "It was stupid and childish."

The earnestness in her eyes left him aching. With his hands gripping the chair arm, he pushed himself closer to the desk. "Congratulations. We agree."

He didn't have to look to know his words hit their mark. "I don't suppose you'd let me explain," she said.

"Would it make any difference?"

"Maybe. No. I don't know."

"Thank you for summarizing everything so clearly." He didn't want to hear any more. Didn't want her orange blossom scent interfering with his anger. "I think you should go," he told her.

Noelle twisted her hat in her hands. This wasn't going at all the way she'd envisioned. Seeing him again reminded her how intimidating a presence he could have when he wanted. It also reminded her how much vulnerability there was beneath the surface. Icy as he sounded, she could see the flashes of pain in his eyes. She wanted to hug him and tell him how amazingly special he was. Only he wouldn't believe her. Not until she cleared the air.

Which was why she stood her ground. She came to explain and make amends for hurting him, and she would.

"I freaked out," she told him. "Saturday was… it felt like a fairy tale with me as Cinderella. You had me feeling all these emotions and suddenly they were too much. I felt scared and guilty and so many things. I needed to get some air."

"All the way back in Michigan? What, New York air not good enough?"

She deserved that. "At first, I only meant to stand outside for a little bit, maybe get a cup of coffee. But then there was this homeless man and these women and… It doesn't matter. Bottom line is, I got scared and ran home where I knew I'd be safe."

"I would have thought you'd find me safe, considering."

"You were. You made me feel incredibly safe. That was part of what freaked me out."

"How reassuring," James replied.

Yeah, listening to what she was saying, Noelle wouldn't buy it either. "I made a mistake," she said.

"No kidding." He shoved the chair away from his desk, causing her to jump. "I told you things I've never shared with anyone," he said, as he stood up. "I opened up to you—and you were the one who pushed me."

Shame at her behavior welled up inside her. "I know," she replied.

"You made me think…" The rest of his sentence died when he ran his hand over his face. "I should have known. When I saw that mantel full of photos, I should have known I couldn't compete with Kevin."

"What?" No, he had it all wrong. "That's not true."

"Noelle, listen to yourself. Thirty seconds ago, you said you felt guilty."

"Yes, but not because of my feelings for Kevin. I felt guilty because I realized Kevin couldn't measure up to you."

Confusion marked his features. "What?"

Noelle took a deep breath. After all his openness, he deserved to know her deepest secret.

"Kevin was a special person," she said. "Every girl in school wanted to date him, so I couldn't believe how lucky I was that he wanted to be with me. Being Kevin Fryberg's girl was the best thing that ever happened to me. Being part of the Frybergs was the biggest dream come true."

"So you've told me," James replied.

"But what I didn't tell you was that Kevin was... he was like the big, wonderful brother I never had."

The confusion deepened. "I don't understand."

"That's the reason I felt so guilty," Noelle said, moving to look out the window herself. "I loved Kevin. I loved our life together, especially when his parents were around. But we never had that phase where we couldn't keep our hands off each other, and I just figured that was because we'd been together for so long. It wasn't until shortly after the wedding that I realized I didn't love him the way a wife should. But by that time, we were committed."

Her fingers ran along the blinds lining the window. "And I had the family I'd always wanted. If he and I ended... So I stuck it out, figuring I'd eventually fall more in love with him. Then Kevin deployed."

And then he died, leaving her the widow of the town hero and forced to keep pretending lest she hurt her surrogate family. She turned so she could study James with her damp gaze. "I didn't know," she whispered.

"Know what?"

"What it felt like to be truly attracted to someone. To have this continual ache in the pit of your stomach because you desperately want them to touch you. Until this past weekend. You made me feel out of control and off-balance and it scared the hell out of me."

"You could have told me," he said. "I would have understood."

"How was I supposed to tell you I could see myself falling for you, when it was those feelings that terrified me?" she replied. "Don't you get it? I was afraid my feelings would blow up in my face and cost me the only family I've ever known."

She waited, watched, while her confession settled over him. After a moment, he ran his hand over his face again and sighed. "If it frightened you, why are you telling me now?"

"Because you deserved to know," she replied. "And because I've realized that family isn't an either-or proposition. Nor is it about being related. It's about love, pure and simple. So long as you have love, you have family."

Risking his rejection, she walked toward him. When she got close enough, she took his hand. "And maybe all that greeting card stuff you despise is a myth, but Christmas can still be wonderful if you're with someone special. Please don't close off the part of you that believes that too."

But James only looked down at their hands. Noelle could take a hint. Foolish of her to think an apology would change much. At least she'd tried. "Anyway, that's what I came to tell you. That you're on the lovable side of the bell curve, and that I wish I hadn't messed up, because there's nothing I would like more than to have been your someone special this Christmas."

"Are you still scared?"

A spark lit in her heart. There was hope in his

voice. He was trying to fight it, but it was there. "Terrified," she replied.

His grip tightened around her fingers. "Me too." Slowly, he lifted his gaze and she saw brightness sparkling in his eyes. "I've never had anyone think I'm special before," he told her.

"I've never been anyone's princess," she told him back.

"So maybe…"

She held her breath and waited.

"Be a shame for you not to see Boston since you flew all the way here," he said.

A hundred-pound weight lifted from her shoulders. She felt like she had the day she met the Frybergs, times ten. "What about my flight home?"

Letting go of her hand, James wrapped an arm around her waist and leaned in until their foreheads touched. "Don't worry," he said. "I know a pilot."

EPILOGUE

Three weeks later

FOR THE LIFE of him, James was never going to get used to those nutcrackers. They were the stuff kids' nightmares were made of. Whistling to himself, he passed under them and headed for the conductor's shack.

"Good afternoon, Ed," he greeted. "How's the train business?"

The conductor blanched. "M-M-Mr. Hammond. We weren't expecting you today. I'm afraid the castle closed early."

"Are you telling me everyone has gone home?" James asked in his sternest voice. "It's only two o'clock."

"Well, it…it is Christmas Eve…"

"James Hammond, stop scaring the employees." Noelle came bouncing out of the conductor's shack wearing a Santa Claus hat and carrying a gold-and-white gift bag. Like it always did when he saw her, James's breath caught in his throat.

"Don't mind him, Ed," she said. "He's not nearly as Grinchy as he'd like people to believe." Rising on tiptoes, she flung her arms around his neck and kissed him soundly. Completely confirming her charge, James kissed her back with equal enthusiasm. Her gift bag crinkled as she wrapped her arms tighter.

"Merry Christmas," she said, smiling. "Nice sweater. You look very festive." He was wearing a red-and-white reindeer jumper purchased at the hotel on his last visit a few days before. One of the advantages of having his own plane was that it made long-distance relationships a lot easier.

"So do you," he replied. "Careful though. If Santa finds out you stole his hat, he'll put you on the naughty list."

"Then we'd better not tell him." Giving him one more kiss, she untangled herself and held out the gift bag. "This is for you. Merry Christmas Eve."

James fingered the red polka-dotted tissue paper peering out from the top of the bag. He might as well have been five again, for the thrill that passed through him.

No, he corrected, a five-year-old wouldn't get this choked up over a simple gift bag. "I thought we agreed to wait and exchange presents tomorrow night when we were alone."

Back in Boston, there was a stack of boxes with Noelle's name on them. More than necessary, probably, but he hadn't been able to help himself. Finally, he understood the joy that came from giving to the people for whom you cared.

"I know," she replied. "This is more of a pre-Christmas present."

Meaning she'd cared enough in return to shop for him. His throat constricted a little more. As far as he was concerned, he already had the best Christmas present in the world standing in front of him.

Her hand came down to rest on his forearm. Shaking off his thoughts, he focused on her shimmering blue gaze instead. "Consider it a small thank-you for asking me if I'd help with next year's window displays," she said. "A very small thank-you. I'm poor from all my Christmas shopping."

"You didn't have to buy anything. Asking for your assistance was a no-brainer. No one is better suited to work on our chain-wide window display extravaganza than you, my little elf." It was true. Hammond's "new direction" involved rolling out Boston's iconic displays on a nationwide basis. The new displays would be more modern and inclusive to reflect the current consumer public, and focus on the message that Christmas was a time for spreading love and goodwill. James was excited for the new project, and for Noelle's involvement since she'd be making frequent trips to Boston. He didn't want to get too ahead of himself, but if things went well he hoped Noelle might someday consider spending even more time in Boston.

Seemed hope had become a habit for him these days.

"Aren't you going to open it?" Noelle asked.

"What?" The gift. He pretended to study the bag. "Considering the size, I'll go out on a limb and say you didn't buy me a drone."

Noelle stuck out her tongue. "Ha-ha-ha. You should be sending that drone a thank-you present. If you hadn't stood in the way, we might never have gotten past the dislike stage."

"True enough."

He shook the bag, only to hear the useless rustling of paper. "It's one of those stuffed Fryer collectibles, isn't it?" After he and Noelle made up, they'd compromised—sort of. Fryer was to be given one last season and then retired with an official ceremony after the first of the year.

"How about you stop guessing and open the package?" Noelle replied. "And don't forget to read the note. It's important."

James did as he was told and discovered a bag full of gingerbread cookies. Two dozen of them.

"I baked them last night," Noelle told him. "In case we get hungry on the way to Belinda's," she said. "Or on the flight tomorrow." They were spending Christmas Eve with Noelle's mother-in-law before flying to Boston for Christmas dinner.

"If you look," she said, "I gave them all little business suits."

Sure enough, she had. "So you can literally bite my head off?"

"Or lick your tummy."

"Sweetheart, you don't need a cookie to do that."

She slapped his arm, and he laughed. Like hope, laughter had also become a regular part of his life.

Funny how quickly things changed. A month ago he'd been utterly alone, and convinced he liked life that way. Now, for the first time in years, he was having a true family Christmas. He was making tentative strides with his father, and with the reappearance of his brother within the family business, it even looked like he and Justin might regain some of the bond they'd lost.

His brother had undergone his own collection of changes this past month. As a result, the two of them had discovered the Hammond family dysfunction had left a mark on both of them. Fortunately, they—and their father—were getting a second chance.

At the end of the day, though, the only person he really needed in his life was the woman in front of him. How right she'd been that day in his office when she said Christmas was wonderful when you had someone special.

And she was special. No longer were the two of them standing on the cusp of something ex-traordinary; they were over-their-heads deep in the middle. And with each passing day, he fell a little deeper. As soon as the timing was right, he planned to let Noelle know he'd fallen in love with her.

"The note," Noelle said prodding him.

Pretending to roll his eyes at her eagerness, he fished out the folded piece of paper. "For our first Christmas together. Made with all my love."

Damn, if he couldn't feel his heart bursting through his chest. "All your love?" he asked.

"Every ounce," she told him. "I love you, James Hammond."

Never had five words filled him with such hope and happiness. They were Christmas, Easter and every holiday in between. "I love you too," he said, pulling her close.

It was going to be a perfect Christmas.

* * * * *